SUPER TROOP

Also by **BRUCE HALE**

Switched

Class Pets:
#1: *Fuzzy's Great Escape*
#2: *Fuzzy Takes Charge*
#3: *Fuzzy Freaks Out*
#4: *Fuzzy Fights Back*

Big Bad Detective Agency

SUPER TROOP

WRITTEN AND ILLUSTRATED BY

BRUCE HALE

SCHOLASTIC PRESS
NEW YORK

Library of Congress Cataloging-in-Publication Data available

ISBN 978-1-338-64599-6

10 9 8 7 6 5 4 3 2 1   22 23 24 25 26

Printed in the Italy   183

First edition, April 2022

Book design by Keirsten Geise

TO MY DAD, FOR STORIES AND INSPIRATION,
AND FOR BEING A TRUE CHARACTER

CONTENTS

1

Robot Pirates

In my defense, it seemed like a fun idea at the time.

I mean, seriously. Who hasn't thought about jumping off a theme park ride to go exploring? Right?

It was the weekend before the last week of school. Our moms had taken me and my best friend, Ignacio "Nacho" Perez, to the Perkiest Place on Earth (aka, Hooten's Family Funland) for an almost-end-of-school celebration. Maybe you go there all the time, but this was kind of a big deal for me because my mom's always working.

So anyway, there we stood, the five of us: Two moms, me and Nacho, and his little sister, Maria, waiting in line for the Prince of Pirates ride. Jolly pirate music blasted from the speakers. Pink cotton candy covered Maria's face and hands, and she was whining about needing the bathroom again.

Then Nacho got an inspiration. I can always tell because one of his eyebrows arches up like a super-villain concocting an evil plan.

"You know," he told his mom, "you guys could take Maria for her bathroom break while we go on the ride."

"Oh, I don't—" Mrs. Perez began.

"Great idea," I chimed in. "We're gonna be in seventh grade soon. We're old enough to ride this by ourselves."

The two moms exchanged a look. If they'd been a cartoon, their thought balloons would've said:

"Pleeeease!" Nacho and I chorused, almost in harmony.

"Neeeed to go potty," Maria added while doing the pee-pee dance.

I could tell my mom was reluctant. She'd been on my case for a while about my not acting responsibly. But it was a scorcher of a day. The wait was another fifteen minutes in the blazing sun, and we were in the Perkiest Place on Earth.

What could possibly go wrong?

The moms locked eyes again, said something else in their Mom ESP, and Mrs. Perez shrugged.

"Okay, honey boy," my mom told me. "But as soon as you finish, meet us right over there." She pointed at the Pirates Landing restaurant across the way. "The *instant* you finish. Understood?"

Nacho and I nodded.

"You've got your phone?"

I patted my pocket. "Right here."

Mom brushed a lock of hair away from my eyes. I kind of hated that she still tried to groom me like I was a little kid (or a baby monkey). But I secretly liked it too.

"All right, have fun, you two," Mom said. "We'll see you in a half hour or so."

"Right over there," added Mrs. Perez, in case we were brain damaged.

Geez, it was like they didn't trust us or something.

So unfair.

Nacho waited until their backs were turned to give me a fist bump.

"That's more like it," he said.

"We are almost teens, after all," I said.

"But still, we never get to do what we want, totally unsupervised."

I watched our moms go and gave a wide grin. Nacho matched it. "Not anymore!" we cried together.

"This is the start of our Summer of Awesomeness!" I declared.

"Yeah, Coop!"

Another fist bump.

By the time we reached the front of the line, after fifteen minutes of shuffling forward like little old men, the excitement had faded. But then, when we climbed into our own boat (shared with four high school girls), it was hard not to grin from ear to ear.

With a rush, the boat took off. As we floated into the mouth of the giant skull, a recorded voice rumbled, "Bewarrrre the Prince of Pirates!" and we disappeared into darkness.

"I love this part," said Nacho.

I opened my mouth to agree, but my words turned into a "wooo!" as the bottom dropped out beneath our boat. My stomach hopped up into my throat. The girls behind us squealed.

Down the rapids we plunged, landing with a splash. The cool spray soothed my sunburned face.

Floating through the pirate camp, I found myself remembering last night's conversation with Mom. "You're old enough to handle it now," she'd said. "Your dad and I have been divorced for almost two years, and it's time I started dating more openly."

My throat went dry at the memory. *Mom, dating?* That wasn't right. The only person she should be dating was Dad.

With an effort, I forced my mind off these thoughts and focused on the summer ahead. It would be perfect. No school. No rules. Just lots of goofing off, watching cartoons, playing video games, eating mint chip ice cream (the best!), and hitting the community pool. And the cherry on top? A one-week cartooning summer camp at the Museum of the Arts, where I'd get to create my first graphic novel.

Woo-hoo!

If only I could come up with the right idea.

Watching the robot pirates, I admired the ride, how perfect and how fun it was. And it all started with a great idea. If I wanted to be a famous cartoonist and animator, I needed to come up with a dope idea like that.

Soon, I promised myself.

I half sang along with the "Yo-ho-ho and a bottle of rum" song.

Nacho nudged me. "I'm bored."

"Seriously? This is the best ride in the park."

Glancing up at the skeletons dangling from the ship's mast, he said, "Yeah, it's an adventure. But it's a *safe* adventure." Nacho looked at me with eyebrows raised.

That look. That look had gotten us into some interesting situations and a fair amount of trouble. Like the summer after fourth grade when he convinced me he'd played so many racing video games that he knew how to drive, and we'd "borrowed" his mom's car. I'd never been grounded before that.

I raked my fingers through my hair. Nacho and I were a great team. Usually, he was the inspiration guy and I was the solutions guy. Nacho identified the problem, and I came up with ways to solve it.

So I wondered, *What would make this ride more fun?*

The boat rounded a curve. Up ahead lay the village where all the robot pirates were looting and pillaging, scaring robot townspeople and stealing gold. Ever since I was little, I'd always wanted to *be* one of those buccaneers.

And that got me thinking . . .

A thrill shivered through me. I glanced over at Nacho. "Want to play pirates?"

A wicked smile curved his lips. "Arrr, matey."

As our boat swung close to the wharf where a robot dog was treating a drunken pirate's peg leg like a chew toy, I gave Nacho the nod. "Let's go!"

Scrambling up onto the boat's prow, we jumped for the dock. Nacho went first, but his leap pushed the boat away from shore. Then I jumped, soaking one leg to the knee and banging the other on the wharf before making it onto dry ground.

"Hey!" cried one of the high school girls. "You can't do that."

"And yet," said Nacho, giving a theatrical bow, "we are."

Cackling like maniacs, we scampered down the dock, my left sneaker squishing with every step. More shouts and hoots erupted behind us. "Someone call security!" a red-faced man shouted. A kid cheered.

We ignored them all.

Swaggering up the street, Nacho and I belted out the "yo-ho" song for all we were worth.

"Arrr," I growled.

"This is so cool!" he crowed.

I felt all tingly and wide-awake. This was what adventure was about—living life to the fullest. I'd always been scared to do something this bold, but not anymore. This was *our* summer.

We approached a fearsome pirate robot brandishing his cutlass. "Hey, handsome," said Nacho. "How about a selfie?"

Fishing my phone from my pocket, I captured the moment. Then Nacho took my picture. Up close, the pirate smelled of machine oil and fifty-year-old plastic. It looked about as realistic as a clothing store mannequin.

Nacho was

right. The ride *was* a tame adventure. But we were making it a real one.

As we turned to go, Nacho kicked our pirate friend in the butt. We were laughing like fools.

From where we stood, the ride was crazy loud. Music blared from hidden speakers just above us, and you could hear the mechanical creaks of the robot pirate on a track as he chased a woman with pearls around and around the town well. You could barely hear the other visitors shouting at us from their boats.

Approaching a storefront, I cupped a hand beside my eyes and peered through the glass. The back wall stood only a foot away, but it was painted to look like the inside of a real store.

All smoke and mirrors. Still, it was pretty cool to be getting a peek behind the curtain at one of my favorite rides.

"Hey, Coop, check this out!" called Nacho.

I joined him by the stone wall with the yowling cat on top. Looking where he pointed, I saw, through a gap between the buildings, a flat black wall, like back-stage at a theater. People in the boats couldn't see it; only us.

"What's that all about?" I asked.

Nacho led the way between the shallow buildings, and as we drew closer, I saw a door with a glowing red EXIT sign above it. Not very piratical looking.

Then I caught another flash of red from the corner of my eye. When I turned, I saw it was the light on a wall-mounted camera.

And the camera was pointed straight at us.

"Hey, chamaco," I said.

Nacho glanced over. "Yeah, chamaco?" (*Chamaco* means something like *kiddo* in Mexican slang. It was our favorite nickname for each other.)

I pointed. "They've got eyes on us."

"Then we better bounce."

Taking one last look around, I spared just enough time for two quick regrets:

One, that we didn't have more time to explore; and

Two, that I hadn't thought there might be cameras.

But which way to escape? We glanced back at the boats, then at the exit. "The door," we said together, and hustled over there at top speed.

Nacho turned the doorknob, and we blinked at the sudden brightness. We'd stepped into a squeaky-clean corridor that looked more like a hospital hallway than a pirate paradise. But the hallway's decor wasn't the first thing I noticed.

No, that would be the two beefy security guards, standing right in front of us with their arms crossed.

"You boys get lost?" rumbled the bigger guard.

"Heh." A nervous laugh escaped me. "I wish we could."

2

Summer of Discipline

Our moms had zero sense of humor about the whole thing. Can you believe it? I mean, just because the security guys made them trek all the way across the park to collect us, and then banned Nacho and me from the park for a year? That's no reason to turn on your own kids.

But they did.

To be honest, I felt pretty bad about it. I really didn't mean to cause Mom any grief. Ever since she and Dad split up, he'd been busy with his other family and she'd been working extra hard to provide for us.

"Do you know how often I take time off for fun?" Mom asked in her shouting-but-not-shouting voice as we rode home in the Perezes' car.

"Um, almost never?" I muttered.

"*Almost never.* And so you decide to ruin my one day off since forever?"

"Um. I'm sorry?" When I thought about it like that, I felt like a complete jerk.

"Was that a question or an apology?" Mom snapped.

I hung my head. "An apology."

During the long silent stretches on the drive home (whenever Maria was napping), I asked myself why I did stuff like that—stuff that got me in trouble and annoyed my parents. The answer? I really didn't know.

Of course, there was a Godzilla-sized list of things I didn't know—the capitals of the world, how to convert inches to millimeters, why Tina Beckman *like*-liked Rob Cahuenga (I mean, *really*)—but not knowing why I did what I did bugged me the most.

I longed for the good old days when Mom and Dad were still together, before they started arguing, before I started getting into trouble. Back then, our biggest issues were deciding on buttered vs. unbuttered popcorn at the movies, or picking the ideal destination for our getaway weekends.

Now *everything* was different.

After a particularly quiet stretch, Mrs. Perez dropped us off at the foot of our driveway. As I waved goodbye to Nacho, we exchanged a look. That look said:

But the truth was, we didn't know if it was worth it, because we didn't yet know our punishment. Let's be honest. This wasn't like hitting a neighbor with a water balloon, or sword fighting with wooden stakes borrowed from a construction site. We had messed with the Perkiest Place on Earth, so we knew the penalty would be serious.

We just didn't know *how* serious.

The first clue? Mom said she'd tell me my punishment after she'd talked to Dad. A weight settled on my chest when I heard that. Usually, if my misbehavior was minor, she'd dish out the penalty first, then let him know afterward. But I guess this screwup was big enough for both parents to get involved.

Lately it felt like, outside of our weekend visits, the only time Dad talked to me was when I was in trouble.

I texted Nacho.

> Me: What's up, chamaco?

Nacho: Grounded, chamaco.

> Me: Bummer. ☹

Nacho: U?

> Me: She's talking to Dad first.

Nacho: Uh-oh.

> Me: No lie.

Nacho: No. Uh-oh, here comes Mom-o and I think sh . . .

> Me: Chamaco?
> Me: Nacho? U there?

No reply. I could only guess that one of his moms had confiscated his phone. A brick settled in my stomach. If they took away his phone, mine couldn't be far behind.

And sure enough . . .

"Cooper Kenichi McCall!" Mom marched into the family room where I was sitting. I could tell she was still steamed because she used my full name—even the middle name that I got from my jii-chan (Japanese grandpa).

She extended her hand. "Your phone. Now."

I dragged myself to my feet, cradling it to my chest. "Thought you were talking to Dad first," I mumbled.

"About your main punishment," she said, her dark eyes hot with anger. "Having a phone is a privilege, and you just lost yours." Mom waggled her fingers, asking for it.

I sighed and set the phone onto her palm.

"But what if—"

"You need to learn to act responsibly and control your impulses," she said. "When you can do that, we'll talk about giving your phone back."

"But, Mom—"

She didn't even stay to hear my objection; she just turned and left the room.

I collapsed onto the sofa. If this was what my parent known as a "soft touch" did, I didn't want to hear what the family disciplinarian had to say.

I sighed.

I was in deep, deep pirate poop.

My next clue about how serious things were came right after dinner, when I was loading the dirty dishes into the dishwasher. Someone rapped on the door and let themselves in. My heart soared, then crashed, because only one person did that.

Dad.

He almost never came inside anymore. For our weekends together, he usually picked me up at the curb and drove me to the house he shared with Shasta McNasty and the Demon Spawn, also known as my almost-stepmother and my twin almost-stepsisters, Piper and Zoey. But here he was, wearing his serious face.

As always, a pang knifed through my heart when I saw them together. Dad was medium height, pale, with sandy brown hair. Mom was short, with golden-brown skin, and that silky, shoulder-length hair that made some people envy Asian women.

They fit so well together. Why weren't they still married?

"Cooper." Dad gave me a curt nod. "Mari." Mom got a friendlier nod. "Where do you want to do this?"

Mom led the way into the family room and told me to sit. She and Dad stood, gazing down like medieval executioners. My nerves were wound tighter than a rubber-band gun.

Despite the sense of doom, though, it cheered me to see the two of them next to each other. It felt comforting, like old times. More than anything, I wanted

Dad back in our house—just not quite like this.

Since moving in with Shasta, he'd changed, and not for the better. He never got to eat chili cheeseburgers anymore, because she was vegan. He never got to do things he loved (like hang out with me) because he was either working or taking care of his girlfriend and her rug rats.

He'd been much better off in the old days. With us.

And Mom had been better too. She shouldn't be dating a bunch of guys who didn't know and appreciate her.

But this family meeting wasn't about them.

With a glance at Mom, Dad led the charge. "We're very disappointed in you, Cooper. We raised you better than this. What on earth were you thinking?"

"Um, that it'd be fun?" I said. *Obviously.* But judging by their expressions, they didn't want to hear that.

"Fun?" said Mom, in the same way that I'd say *Brussels sprouts.*

My eyes dropped to a thread poking out of the frayed fabric on the chair's arm. I toyed with it. "I—I guess I wasn't thinking."

"And that's the whole problem," said Dad. "You're almost a teenager. This acting out isn't cute anymore. Keep it up, and you'll land in serious trouble. When I worked for the Public Defender's Office, I saw those kids in court all the time."

Mom waggled her index finger. "You need to learn discipline, Cooper. This can't go on."

I'd heard this all before—and the suspense was killing me.

"Okay, so you're taking away my phone," I blurted. "What else?"

"Excuse me?" Dad's voice had some steel in it.

I straightened. "I messed up and I have to be more disciplined, I get it. Just skip ahead and tell me my punishment."

"You want your punishment, smart guy?" said Dad. "You've got it: You're grounded."

"Grounded? But what about—"

Mom's hands patted the air. "Obviously you're still going to school for your last week."

"But straight home afterward," said Dad. "No hanging out at Ignacio's house."

"Nacho," I corrected him. Had Dad forgotten *everything* since he moved out?

"And no trips to the arcade," Dad said.

I slumped back against the armchair. Being grounded stank. But things could be worse. I'd toughed out being grounded once before, and I'd do it again.

"And . . ." said Mom.

"And?" *Uh-oh.*

Her lips tightened. "You're joining a Boy Rangers troop. Maybe they can teach you some self-control."

I shot upright. "Boy Rangers?"

"That's right," she said.

"But, but that's for dorks and rejects. Noooo."

Dad's eyes were flinty. "Would you prefer to skip your cartooning camp?"

My head swiveled so fast, it almost came off. "You're not serious."

"As a heart attack," said Dad. "Unless you join the

Rangers, and demonstrate some responsibility and impulse control, you're not attending that camp."

I felt gut-punched.

Unable to catch my breath, I looked from him to her.

A slight shift in Mom's eyes let me know that this was Dad's idea. "You've got a choice," she said. "I've heard good things about the Rangers."

"It's for little boys," I moaned. "I'm in *middle school*."

Dad put on his courtroom face. "It's for boys from eleven to fifteen, according to their website. Lots of high school kids join. Some troops even go hiking, and I know you like getting out in nature."

Of course I liked getting outdoors. Taking nature walks together was one of the special things Dad and I shared. But that wasn't the point here.

"The Rangers are massive dweebs," I said. "Heck, they even wear *uniforms*."

"So?" said Dad. "What's your decision?"

Gritting my teeth, I growled, "Ugh. This is so unfair."

Dad's phone chimed with an incoming text, and he glanced at it. Probably Shasta. His other family wanted him back, and my ten minutes were up.

I heaved a huge sigh. "Fine. I'll be a stupid Boy Ranger."

Anything was better than giving up my dream and missing out on the chance to become a real cartoonist.

"Wise choice," said Mom, smoothing her shirtfront. "And you'll be pleased to know that Nacho will be joining you too."

"Nacho?"

She offered a tight smile. "Yes, his moms actually came up with the idea. That way, you'll each know someone in the troop."

My head fell back against the chair. *Oh, great.* We'd both suffer. They say misery loves company? This would be like having company while being tortured on the rack. Distracting, but not exactly comforting.

Dad tucked his phone into his pocket. "You'd better take this seriously, son. I've let the Museum of the Arts know that there's a chance you might not be attending their camp. They'll only hold your place for another month. I expect to see progress."

Yikes.

My dad is a serious guy—this was no idle threat. Seemed like his sense of humor had been AWOL ever since he and Mom split up, and he was becoming a different person. I missed goofing off with him, going on nature walks, and watching old *Star Wars* movies together. I missed the spicy smell of his aftershave.

But all I said when he made his excuses a minute later and headed out the door was "Bye, Dad."

Mom watched him go with a complicated expression on her face. Was she missing the old days too?

I bit my lip. Right then I decided something.

They wanted this to be my Summer of Discipline? Fine. I wanted this to be their Summer of Getting Back Together.

We'd see whose summer it turned out to be.

3

Ancient Pillow Fighters

The following week turned out to be pretty much as Dad had described it. I went to school, I came home, I ate, I slept.

Rinse, repeat.

Over and over.

When Mom was still at work, I tried searching for my hidden phone. No luck. I guessed she'd learned a thing or two after the last time she confiscated it. Dang.

My homework was minimal. It was the last week of sixth grade, after all. What were they going to do, flunk me for skipping math homework?

In my free time, I drew characters from my favorite graphic novels (especially *Bone* and *Usagi Yojimbo*, an awesome comic about a samurai rabbit). When I wasn't doing that, I played video games, watched YouTube videos on our home computer, and dreamed of freedom.

Somehow, the week limped to an end. Walking home on the last day of school was usually pure excitement. You felt lighter than air, like you'd swallowed a helium balloon, and the whole summer stretched out before you, pure and perfect.

Not this time.

Nacho and I trudged down the sidewalks, discussing the terms of our imprisonment.

"You get your phone back yet?" I asked.

He shook his head.

"Me neither."

We trudged on.

"Any word on how long you'll be grounded?" asked Nacho.

"Maybe another couple weeks. You?"

He lifted a shoulder. "My moms both said that after a knuckleheaded stunt like that, I'll be grounded until I'm seventy. They said I'll come over to your house, all toothless, like, 'You wanna pillow fight, Coop?'" This last bit Nacho did in an old-man-type voice. He was good with voices.

I cracked up in spite of myself. "And I'll be like, 'Take that! Ooh, my back!'"

We sobered up a little. "You think they really mean it?" I asked.

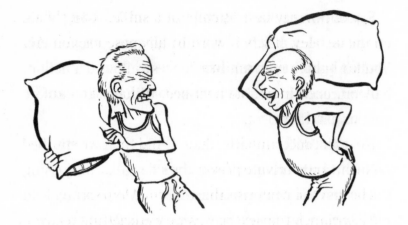

Nacho just shrugged.

At the corner where he normally split off to go to his house, we stopped.

"So," said Nacho.

"So," I said.

"Boy Rangers tomorrow?"

"Ugh. Don't remind me."

He rolled his eyes. "We suffer together, chamaco. Hey, if it gets too boring, I'll teach you some curse words in Spanish."

"But I already know—"

A loud honking cut me off. We turned to see a high school kid in a red sports car zoom past, screeching, "Yeehaw!"

"At least someone's excited about the end of school," said Nacho. "See you tomorrow?"

I gave him my best attempt at a smile. "Can't wait, chamaco. Hey, here's a word in Japanese for you. My jii-chan taught me: *gambatte*."

After repeating it, Nacho asked, "What's it mean?"

"Hang in there."

He nodded. "Gambatte, dude." And then we shuffled off to our own private prisons.

The first bad news was the uniform. Mom sprang it on me after lunch the next day as we were getting ready to leave, by thrusting a big plastic bag into my hands.

"You want me to take out the trash?" I said.

She gave me the long-suffering look that greeted most of my jokes. "It's your uniform. Put it on."

Opening the bag, I saw the dreaded khaki shirt, olive-green pants and optional shorts, necker-chief, and cheesy cap of the Boy Rangers. The cap even sported a patch featuring the troop's bucktoothed beaver mascot, Bucky.

Not to brag, but I could draw a better mascot with my eyes closed.

"Mom, there's still time to change your mind. We

can just tell Dad I went to the meeting, and then go to the movies instead. Heck, I'd even watch one of your rom-coms."

She crossed her arms. "You do have a choice."

"I do? Great. Then I choose not to go."

"A choice between Boy Rangers and missing your cartooning camp," she said.

My shoulders slumped. "Just kill me now," I muttered.

Mom gave me a gentle shove. "Okay, Drama Boy. Go suit up."

The thing fit okay, at least. I chose the long pants; no way could I appear in public in those shorts. Slipping on my tennies, I joined Mom in the front hallway.

"Where's your cap?" she asked, looping her purse strap over one shoulder.

"Do I have to?" I asked.

When she nodded, I fetched the thing from my room and put it on. During our walk to the car, I felt like a dog wearing the Cone of Shame. I just hoped no cute girls saw me like this. Instant death to my reputation. (Not that I had any reputation, but still.)

As if the uniform wasn't bad enough, after we met

up with Nacho and Mrs. Perez in the school parking lot, our moms kept walking with us. Like we were snot-nosed kindergartners on the first day of school or something. (Or like they knew we'd try to bolt.)

My face felt hot. I was probably blushing redder than a stop sign.

The Boy Rangers met at the picnic tables outside my middle school's cafeteria. As we approached the raggedy-looking group, I hoped nobody I knew saw us. Over on the basketball courts, a handful of regular kids were playing hoops.

I kept my cap brim pulled low.

A measly six boys clambered around the tables, laughing, goofing off, giving each other noogies, and so forth.

I turned to Nacho. "How many Rangers in a troop?"

Shaking his head, he said, "Looks like this one's on life support."

One kid knelt over a patch of dying grass with a magnifying glass, trying to start a fire (or maybe roast a bug). Another was throwing his pocketknife at a target between his partner's feet. A third one had jammed his pinkie in his nostril up to the second joint, mining for boogers.

None of them wore a complete uniform. None of

them demonstrated the "self-control" we were supposed to learn.

Nacho and I traded a look. *This* was our summer activity?

"Do you see any discipline here?" he muttered.

"Zero," I whispered back. "Easiest punishment ever." My spirits lifted a bit.

Our moms steered us toward a walrus-shaped white man who leaned against the outdoor stage, finishing a burger and tapping away on his cell phone. As we

approached, I noticed the muffin top bulging over his belt, the too-small shorts cutting into his legs, the beard stubble, and his puffy, ruddy face. When he looked up, his eyes were bloodshot.

"Yes?" he said vaguely.

Nacho's mom pushed forward and introduced us. "Our sons are here to join the troop."

Walrus Man's expression cleared. "Oh, right, right. The new kids." Popping the last bite of burger into his maw, he spoke through a full mouth. "I'm Troopmaster Randy Brozny. Welcome to our summer program, boys."

Nacho and I nodded. The man's breath smelled like an aquarium—an aquarium that'd just had a hamburger dropped into it.

A loud pop and an "Ow!" caught my attention. One of the Rangers was shooting his BB gun at a can, and it looked like he'd nailed another boy in the butt.

Mr. Brozny just grunted. "You got their paperwork?"

My mom dug in her purse, handing my form to the man. Mrs. Perez did the same for Nacho.

Wiping a greasy paw on his belly, Troopmaster Brozny took the papers, barely glanced at them, and grunted again. "Fine, fine." He snapped the sheets onto his clipboard, giving our moms a cheesy smile. "Now, if you *ladies* will excuse us, it's just about time for some manly man stuff."

Waddling off, he took the BB gun away from a skinny older kid whose face was a Jackson Pollock painting, if Pollock had painted with zits.

My mom drew me aside. "I know you don't want to be here, honey boy."

I blew out some air in a *pfff*. "Oh, you think?"

"It's for your own good," she continued, straightening my cap. "Try to have some fun."

Then she and Mrs. Perez took off, and we were left to deal with whatever *Lord of the Flies*–type situation they'd dumped us in. Although Nacho and I broke the rules from time to time, we never did anything that would hurt people. It seemed like these guys didn't have those same limits.

Nacho edged closer as he eyed the redheaded kid flipping his knife into the ground. "What the heck?" he muttered.

"Let's stick together," I murmured. "I'm sensing a disturbance in the Force."

Walrus Man blew a silver whistle that hung from his neck. "Gather round, kids. Let's get started."

No one paid him any attention. Knife Boy went on flipping, the Firebug had finally gotten a little flame burning in the grass, and a kid who looked like the Incredible Hulk's son had another boy in a headlock.

"Come on, let's move it!" shouted the troopmaster. "I'm not doing this for my health, you know." When they still didn't respond, he walked over and herded the kids toward the first two picnic tables. Grudgingly, they obeyed.

"Hey, uh—" said Nacho, pointing to the pyromaniac's fire, which was spreading.

Rolling his eyes, the kid went back and stomped it out. He looked part Asian like me, with intense serial-killer eyes behind his heavy glasses.

When everyone had finally settled down, Mr. Brozny picked up his clipboard and cleared his throat.

"Welcome, Troop Nineteen. As you can see, we have a couple of new Rangers today. Please welcome . . ."

He glanced down at the clipboard, searching for our names, which he'd already forgotten. The other boys craned their necks, staring at us like some exotic creatures they might like to add to their menu.

"Ah, Ignacio and Cooper," said Walrus Man at last.

I spoke up before he could continue. "Coop," I said, jerking a thumb toward my chest.

"Huh?"

"And Nacho," said Nacho.

Hulk Jr. snickered. "Nacho?"

"Yeah," said my friend. "What's your name, Beef Burrito?"

The big kid grunted, not sure whether to get up and pound Nacho or just laugh. Zit Face whispered in his ear, and Hulk Jr. settled down.

"Okay," said the troopmaster, making a note on his clipboard. "Two boys who don't like their names. Anyway, make Coop and, um, Nacho, welcome."

The Firebug gave me a nod, and a chubby boy reached out for a handshake, mumbling, "José."

"Hey, gang, let's teach them our Boy Rangers song," said Mr. Brozny, all teeth and fake enthusiasm. Honestly, the guy looked like he'd rather be nursing his obvious hangover in a dark cave somewhere. But with another toot on the whistle, he launched into the song. José and another guy sang with enthusiasm, but the rest lip-synched, messed with their phones, or looked bored.

As I heard more of the song, I understood why.

Rangers, Rangers, we're the best,
Twice as good as all the rest.
Brave and loyal, strong and true,

Tough enough to see it through.
Rangers always stay prepared,
Rangers bold are never scared.
Reverent and cheerful too,
We are Rangers through and through!

The song had a second verse, but just like "Amazing Grace" and "Silent Night," almost nobody knew what it was. The singing petered out. The Rangers regarded each other self-consciously.

"Well, it's no 'Hey Jude,'" whispered Nacho, who's a big fan of geezer rock like the Beatles.

"Not even the 'Hokey Pokey,'" I muttered back. Inside, I brooded. This group wasn't just embarrassing; it was mortifying. True, it did look like our time in Boy Rangers would be a total cruise. That was a plus.

But if they thought they'd ever get *me* to sing that dumb song, they were seriously mistaken.

Troopmaster Brozny fetched a box from the stage and pulled out a length of rope. "Okay, Rangers. Today we'll work on our knot-tying skills. Let's review. Who can show us how to tie a square knot?"

The other boys avoided catching his eye. No one raised a hand.

"Anybody?" said Walrus Man, in a pleading tone.

"Come on, a couple of you have been Rangers for two years. Surely someone knows how to tie a square knot?"

"I can do it," said a female voice, strong and clear.

We all twisted around. Behind us stood three girls in khaki-and-green uniforms.

"Bridget," said the troopmaster, in the same tone you'd use for discussing a worrisome wart. "I hoped— er, thought you'd gotten lost."

"A Ranger can always find her way, day or night," said the tallest of the three, a pale girl with long reddish hair and a determined chin.

"Look, it's no use dressing up your friends as Rangers," said Mr. Brozny. "I told you last time, you belong in the Girl Scouts."

"Girl Scouts!" The shorter girl with chopped-off black hair barked out a laugh. "Are you saying girls can't be Rangers? That we don't have the grit?"

The troopmaster looked as perplexed as a hound dog on roller skates, suddenly unsure of his footing. "Um. I'm confused. You two ladies are . . . ?"

"Your newest troop members," said the third girl, who was cute, caramel-skinned, and had an infectious smile.

All the guys' jaws dropped.

Nacho turned to me. "Boy Rangers just got a whole lot more interesting."

4

Soda Fireworks

"But that's not—girls aren't supposed to—I mean . . ." Poor Mr. Brozny never quite recovered from the shock. But the rest of us were eager to meet the newest recruits.

The tall girl introduced herself as Bridget Click, then ended up teaching knot tying by default after an older boy with a unibrow challenged her, "Bet you can't tie a clove hitch."

While they competed and we cheered them on, the troopmaster tried in vain to call the troop sponsor, the district board, and various bigwigs to complain about the new arrivals. Apparently, Boy Rangers had recently lost a lawsuit and was being forced to admit girls. Much to Brozny's dismay, Bridget was the first in our town. And as I quickly learned, Bridget's smiley friend was Tavia Jackson, and the one with the short black hair was Frankie Patel.

They laughed when their friend showed Agent Unibrow that she could tie a sheepshank and he couldn't. The boy stomped off to the bathroom in a huff, probably to cry his eyeballs out.

"Next time, don't assume you're better just because you're up against a girl!" Bridget called after him.

Tavia gave her a high five.

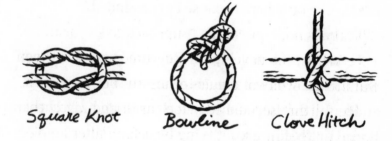

Square Knot   Bowline   Clove Hitch

A few minutes later, I was sitting atop one of the tables, trying to make sense of the bowline knot, when Frankie plopped down beside me.

"What's the deal with Brozny?" she said.

"Um," I said, extremely aware of her warm arm right next to mine. "He, uh—I haven't figured him out."

She cocked her head, humor sparkling in her fawn-colored eyes. "Really? He doesn't seem like an international man of mystery to me."

Glancing over, I caught Mr. Brozny leaning a hand

on the stage, sputtering into the phone, ignoring us completely.

I shrugged. "Me neither. But I only joined fifteen minutes before you."

"Oh, so you're a big help."

"Yeah," I said. "Mr. Helpful, that's me."

She smirked.

Keeping my attention on undoing my tangled knot, I said, "I'm only here because I'm grounded."

"Okay."

"Truth is, I'm not big on Boy Rangers. But if you want to know about comics or anime, I'm your man." Suddenly, that seemed way too flirty, and my cheeks burned. "Uh, I mean . . ."

Frankie cocked her head, surveying me with narrowed eyes. "Oh yeah? What's your favorite comic?"

I glanced over at Nacho, but he was part of the crowd hanging around Tavia. Frankie and I were on our own. "You've probably never heard of it," I said.

"Try me."

"It's *Bone: Out from Boneville*, by—"

"Jeff Smith," said Frankie. "Those books rock."

My eyes widened. "I'm impressed."

"Why, because girls don't like comics?"

"No," I said, blushing again, even though that had been my first thought. "It's, um, it's just, not everyone knows—"

Fweeeet!

A whistle blast saved me from putting my foot even deeper into my mouth.

Red-faced, Mr. Brozny glared at everyone. "All right, I can't seem to reach anyone with a lick of sense, but we'll sort this out on Monday."

Frankie and I traded puzzled looks.

"In the meantime, let's see what you Rangers are made of," said the troopmaster. "Take three laps around the field."

"What?" I said.

"Now?" asked the Firebug.

"Jogging?" said Hulk Jr., like someone had asked him to sleep on My Little Pony sheets.

"Yes, jogging," said the troopmaster. "That's if you new recruits think you can handle it." As he eyed the three girls, his expression looked almost hopeful.

Frankie bristled. "I'm the fastest forward on my soccer team. I can run rings around anyone here."

Mr. Brozny's face fell. "Oh. Okay. Well, what's everyone waiting for?"

The Rangers exchanged doubtful glances. If we'd wanted to run laps, we would've signed up for summer sports.

Tavia stared wide-eyed at something to one side of the tables.

"Scared of a little exercise, girl?" Brozny chuckled.

"It's, ah . . ." The new Ranger couldn't seem to speak.

"What now?" said the troopmaster. "Spit it out, girl."

"F-f-fire!" cried Tavia, pointing.

I stood up on the bench for a better look. Turned out, the pyromaniac was as sloppy a fire-putter-outer as he was an excellent fire-starter. Smoke billowed in the sunshine, and the flames burned merrily, spreading wider and wider.

"*FIRE!*" screamed Zit Face, like Tavia hadn't just said that.

"Thanks," I said. "We noticed."

"Now what do we do about it?" asked Nacho.

Bridget Click jumped into action like she'd been doing this all her life.

"We need water, sand, or blankets," she barked. "Come on, people. Kelvin Chang!" Bridget stabbed a finger at the Firebug.

"Me?" said Kelvin.

"Go find the janitor."

"The *janitor?*" He sounded disappointed, like he wanted to stay and see how much of the field would burn.

"To get him to turn on the sprinklers," said Bridget. "Go!"

"I'll call 9-1-1," Nacho volunteered, reaching for Kelvin's phone. "Um, what's the number again?"

"Nine-one-one!" Frankie and I shouted together.

"Right," said Nacho. "I knew that."

Bridget clapped her hands. "Everybody, let's move it!"

As Mr. Brozny gaped like a petrified walrus, the rest of us lurched into action. Hulk Jr. and José grabbed the massive cooler full of ice and soft drinks. Staggering over to the edge of the grass, they flung its contents over the fire, sending ice, soda cans, and cooler lid flying into the flames.

"Take cover!" I cried, jumping off the table and sheltering behind it. "Get back!"

"Why?" asked Hulk Jr.

"It's gonna blow," I said.

José scratched his cheek. "You're kidding?"

"Trust me, I know what happens when you throw a soda can into a fire."

Light dawned in their eyes, and the big guy hustled back behind the picnic tables, followed closely by José. Everyone else cringed, waiting. The seconds ticked past as the fire spread. Five . . . ten . . . fifteen.

Hulk Jr. stood. "No boom-boom. You pranking me?"

I held up both hands. "I swear."

And then:

POW! Pop-pop-pa-POW!

Fifteen or twenty soda cans went off like fireworks, blasting into the air and spraying fountains of refreshing beverages. At the sound, Hulk Jr. hit the concrete. Everyone else ducked.

When the soda fireworks stopped, the flames still burned. I cast about for anything that would help control them.

Rope.

The troop flag.

Brozny's clipboard.

All seemed equally useless. Then I spotted the picnic blanket the troopmaster had draped across the front of the stage where he was currently leaning his wide behind.

Nacho was still on the phone. I glanced over at Frankie. "Give me a hand?"

"With what?" she asked.

Dashing over to the stage, I whisked the blanket out from behind Brozny's butt. "Grab the other side," I said. "Maybe we can smother the fire."

Frankie snatched one end of the heavy woolen blanket. Moving as close as we dared, we whapped it on the ground over and over, trying to suffocate the flames.

The heat beat against us like a live thing. Sweat poured down my face and arms, and I was glad I'd worn long pants.

Finally, just as wailing sirens announced the fire trucks' arrival, a jet of water sprayed onto the flames. From somewhere around the school, Zit Face had located a hose and hooked it up. By the time the firefighters in their tan-and-yellow uniforms had reached us, the grass fire was pretty much out.

I coughed from the smoke. Digging in her book bag, Frankie passed me a water bottle. "Thanks," I croaked, gulping it down.

Nacho clapped me on the shoulder. "Nice job, chamaco."

"It wasn't just me." I caught Frankie's eye. "Group effort."

She grinned. A little shadow crossed Nacho's face when he saw this, but it was gone almost before I noticed.

The firefighters handled the mop-up, putting out the last hot spots, while their leader asked us what had happened. I noticed that no one mentioned Kelvin the Firebug frying ants or whatever with that magnifying glass. Maybe because he looked so mournful. (Although I wasn't sure if he felt bad for starting the fire or bad because it got put out.)

All in all, it was an eventful first meeting.

At long last, the fire trucks pulled away. Mr. Brozny had forgotten all about our running laps, so he just sent us home with a curt "Meeting's over."

And that was that. Without ceremony, the Rangers packed up and plodded off toward the parking lot. When I glanced back, the troopmaster was once again muttering to himself, pecking away at his cell phone, and looking like he might blow a gasket. Not for the first time, I wondered if an adult like him should be in charge of a bunch of teens and tweens.

As Nacho fell in beside me for the walk home, he shook his head. "Whoa, chamaco."

"Yup," I agreed. "It's going to be a long, long summer."

He raised a finger. "But not," he said, "a boring one!"

5

The Demon Spawn Twins

Since she was on call, Mom ended up working a shift at the hospital that afternoon. That meant I had a couple of hours alone to mull over my encounter with the Boy Rangers. It sure wasn't what I'd expected.

On the one hand, yes, the group was still ultra-lame, it interfered with my summer plans, and the troop leader stank like a dumpster burrito. But on the other hand . . .

GIRLS!

Plus, if Brozny was this incompetent, Nacho and I would be able to cruise through our days of punishment (assuming we didn't get burned up first).

I didn't know what to think.

Mom breezed in just before dinner, bearing salad and a pizza from Pizzanista!—my favorite spot—with deep-dish crust and Thai seasonings. You wouldn't think a pad Thai pizza would rock, but this one did.

I snagged a slice as soon as she set the box down on the table. For a little while, we ate in easy silence, and I forgot about my Prince of Pirates mishap and my punishment, about my parents' divorce and my plans to reunite them. We were just a boy and his mom, eating pizza, enjoying summer.

Until . . .

"How was your first day of Boy Rangers, honey?"

Gulp. "Um, it was okay."

Parental questions can be tricky. Sometimes, they don't really want to know the answer, but they have to ask because they're your parents. Other times, they want the whole truth.

"Just okay?" she asked. "Tell me more."

She wanted truth? I'd give her truth.

Wiping my mouth, I said, "Well, it probably won't be called *Boy* Rangers much longer." I explained about the three girls who'd joined after me and Nacho.

"Very progressive." She nodded approvingly. "It's about time. Girls can do anything boys can do."

Mouth full again, I nodded.

"And how's your troop leader," she asked, "Mr. Brozny?"

I rolled my eyes. "The worst."

"Oh, you're just saying that."

"No, he literally is. He let a guy practically burn down the athletic field, and then just watched while we all ran around trying to put it out. The fire department had to help."

"I'm sure he was just—" My words finally sank in. "A *fire?*"

I lifted another slice. "Yup. The whole school could've burned down. It was pretty scary." I didn't mention how I'd kind of enjoyed the excitement.

"He let someone start a *fire?*" she repeated, louder. "Like a campfire?"

"Nope, in the grass. Either Mr. Brozny wasn't paying attention or he didn't care."

Mom gripped her napkin. "Was anyone burned?"

Although tempted to stretch the truth, I stuck to the facts. "Nobody got hurt, unless you count Brozny's picnic blanket." I sat back and watched to see how she'd take it. Would I get lucky?

"That's—" Mom opened her mouth and closed it again.

I shrugged. "Hey, if you want to take me out of the Rangers, I totally get it. It's not safe."

But inside, two parts of me were at war:

Mom wasn't born yesterday. (Obviously, because I was almost thirteen.) She got ahold of herself, took a deep breath, and said, "Well, they *are* supposed to teach you how to start a fire. And you worked together to put it out? That sounds pretty Ranger-y to me."

That wasn't what I'd expected.

"Uh, don't you want to get Dad over here to talk about it?" I asked. *And maybe remember how much you miss each other?*

She glanced at the stove clock. "I might call him after dinner."

"So . . . I'm out?" I tried not to sound too gleeful.

Mom speared some salad on her fork. "I'm thinking we should give it at least one more meeting."

Again, I felt that weird mix of disappointment and relief. "But Dad—"

"We'll see what he thinks," she said. "For now, let's focus on the important stuff." In her best Cookie Monster voice, she said, "Pizza!"

This conversation wasn't over. But what red-blooded American boy would argue about pizza?

In the end, my parents decided that I would give the Rangers another shot. (As usual, I didn't get a vote.) And to make things worse, they reached their decision over the phone. Apparently, a flaming athletic field wasn't a serious enough problem to pry Dad away from his other family for a visit.

If I wanted to get my parents back together and improve their lives, I'd have to find another way.

The week passed boringly enough. On Tuesday, we had another Rangers meeting with Brozny, and he seemed about as happy to be there as a tomcat in a hot tub. He griped endlessly about how the Boy Rangers were on the wrong track, and headed for disaster, and blah, blah, blah. I got the distinct idea that the man was an old-school sexist oinker. (Something that was seconded by Frankie.)

He didn't even have us do Ranger-type activities. We just sat around, yakking or reading the dumb handbook until it was time to go. On Thursday, Brozny didn't even show up. (Nor did Agent Unibrow, who also seemed to have a problem with girls in the troop.) After Bridget called the district office to complain, they sent someone to keep an eye on us until the meeting time was over.

Bridget was livid. This wasn't what she'd signed up for. Where were the wilderness challenges, the skill building, the adventure? Nacho and I, on the other hand, were totally chill. At least the promise of harsh discipline seemed to have faded to nothing, and nobody got stabbed or burned.

All in all, I guess there were a few worse ways to spend my time.

But of course, I was still grounded. The days were getting warmer, but I couldn't go to the pool or goof off with Nacho. Instead, my dad's mom, Nana C, came to babysit me while Mom was working. (She lived just down the street.)

I loved my grandma, but seriously? A babysitter? What was I, a little kid or something?

Come Friday afternoon, it was time for my weekend with Dad. I felt like a prisoner out on parole. *What's that blue thing up above me, the sky?* I knew I'd feel even better when we went for a nature walk the next day.

Same as always, Dad pulled his car up to the curb and honked, and same as always, Nana C said, "I raised that boy better than that."

Giving her a kiss on the cheek, I hoisted my overnight bag onto one shoulder. "And now he's too old to spank."

She arched an eyebrow. "Don't bet on it."

When I piled into the passenger seat, Dad smiled at me and lifted a finger in the universal sign for *just a sec*. "No," he told the windshield. "That's not what that clause covers. No, we've discussed that. You won't— fine, then. Talk with your client. Okay."

As I often thought when I saw this, the line separating some random nutjob talking to himself from a lawyer chatting over his AirPods was a very slim one. "Okay, bye." He tapped a button on his steering wheel, cutting off the call.

"Work?" I asked.

"Work," he said.

Of course it was. My dad was always busy, and these days it seemed to be getting even worse—especially with Shasta's two little monsters running around their house, sucking up all his spare minutes. Back when he and Mom were together, he always had time for me.

"So, where are we going tomorrow?" I asked. "I was thinking maybe Inspiration Point or San Anselmo."

The hills behind Santa Romina were crisscrossed with trails. Although he worked as a lawyer, Dad knew all kinds of cool facts about plants and animals, which made our hikes fascinating.

For example, did you know that horned toads can squirt blood from their eyeballs? So cool.

Dad made That Face. "Sorry, buddy. I wish I could. I'll be tied up with this contract all weekend."

I crossed my arms, slumping in my seat. "You never have time for me."

Pulling away from the curb, Dad shot me a glance. "That's not true, Cooper. Things have been crazy at work lately, but—"

"Yeah, yeah. Work, work, work, I know . . ."

The cell phone's ring interrupted me, and Dad tapped the steering wheel again. "McCall here. Yes. No, Yolanda, I left those files at the office." With an apologetic wink, he dove into another conversation, which didn't end until we pulled into his driveway.

I sighed, shouldered my overnight bag, and followed him up the walkway.

His new place was bigger than the house he used to share with Mom and me. But somehow, not big enough for me to have my own room for my every-other-weekend visits. Instead, I bunked in his office on the sofa bed, with a file cabinet and inspirational posters looming over me. (Ever tried falling asleep with FORTUNE FAVORS THE BRAVE staring down at you? It's a lot of pressure.)

We had a decent enough dinner that night, some kind of vegan taco salad. But every time I tried to catch a little of my dad's attention, either Shasta McNasty or her Devil Spawn would interfere.

"Hey, Dad, I was thinking about starting my graphic novel this summer before I go to camp," I said.

"Good idea," he said. "You've certainly got the talent to—"

"Daddy-Daddy-Daddy!" said one of the twins. (Piper, I was pretty sure.)

He turned to her. "Yes, princess?"

"Guess what?" she said.

Dad smiled indulgently. "What, Piper?"

"I saw . . . I saw . . . a ewephant!"

"Is that so? On the TV?"

Piper shook her head, her blond pigtails whipping her face. "Inna backyard."

Dad chuckled.

I tried again. "So I can't decide whether to draw

animals or human characters, you know? Like in *Maus*, they—"

"Daddy-Daddy-Daddy!" said the other twin. "I saw . . . I saw . . . a wion!"

He gave her the same dopey grin. "A lion? Really? What was it doing?"

Zoey smiled broadly. "Eating cake!" Clapping her hands, she threw back her head and laughed like she'd said the funniest thing in the world.

I shook my head. No way could I compete with that level of cuteness.

Misinterpreting, Zoey patted my hand. "Cooph, I weawy did see a wion."

I sighed. As adorable as the twins were, I didn't fit in here. They were Shasta's kids from her first marriage. They were *her* family. And they'd hijacked my dad, taken away the things he loved to do.

I got that Dad felt sorry for Shasta when her sleaze-bag husband ran off, leaving her with two infants. But did he have to move in with her before the ink dried on his divorce papers? Couldn't he have just sent a sympathy card?

Although half of my friends went from house to house between their divorced parents like I did, I'd never gotten used to it. Even after almost two years, I still felt like that divorce had split more than my parents' relationship. It had split me down the middle.

Saturday morning, I didn't even get to sleep in. The Devil Spawn Twins shattered my sleep by bursting into the room at some ungodly hour. Within seconds, they were bouncing on the sofa bed shouting, "Pamcakes, pamcakes!"

Half-awake, I swiped at the nearest one with my pillow (not hard—I'm not an idiot). "Go 'way," I mumbled.

"Cooph wike pamcakes?" the other one asked.

"Later," I said, rolling over to face the sofa side of the bed. I should've known that wouldn't work.

Next thing I knew, sticky little fingers were tapping my forehead. "Pam-cakes! Pam-cakes! PAM-CAKES!" my almost-stepsisters chanted.

"Stop it!" I roared.

Both girls clammed up right away, backing off and watching me with huge eyes. Great, now I'd terrified a couple of innocent toddlers. Maybe Mom was right about my needing to learn discipline.

I apologized for yelling and rolled out of bed.

And so the day began.

Hours later, after a lunch of Shasta's gluten-free (try taste-free) broccoli casserole, it was time to psych myself up for another round of Boy Rangers. I figured I'd at least enjoy a little alone time with my dad on the way to the meeting, but when I stepped out of the bathroom in my dorky uniform, he barely glanced up from the computer screen.

"Sorry, bud," he said, "I won't be able to take you."

Relief bloomed in my chest. "Really? Oh, well. I'll find something else to do." I began pulling off my neckerchief.

"Shasta can drive you," he said.

Oh, great.

He raised his voice. "Hey, sweetie, can you take Cooper to the Rangers meeting?"

She drifted up to the doorway in a cloud of blond hair and honeysuckle perfume. "Sure thing, hon. If you can keep an eye on the girls?"

I saw the flicker in Dad's eyes, but he said, "Absolutely."

He knew as well as I did that no work would get done while he chased around after two three-year-olds. He might as well have driven me himself. But once Dad makes a decision, he's harder to budge than a sumo wrestler in concrete booties.

Reluctantly, I headed for the door.

The ride with my almost-stepmom wasn't so bad— no worse than lying on a bed of nails butt naked. She'd always made an effort to be nice to me, even though she clearly had no clue about dealing with almost-teenage boys. I tried staring straight ahead and keeping quiet, but did that work?

Fat chance. Shasta seemed to feel that this was Quality Bonding Time.

"So, how's your summer shaping up so far?" she chirped.

"I'm grounded."

She blinked. "Oh, right. Well . . ." Searching around

for another topic, Shasta said, "Are you enjoying the Boy Rangers? My dad used to be a Ranger, and he loved his time with them."

All the more reason to avoid it, I thought.

"Pretty lame so far," I said.

She took a long breath. "Coop, I'm not your enemy."

This made me actually turn to look at her. "What?"

Shasta negotiated a careful left turn before continuing. "I'm not trying to replace your mom."

"That's good, because I—"

"Already have a mom," she finished. "I know. But I'm hoping that since we're practically family, we can at least be friends."

I stared forward at the middle school up the street, willing it closer. "Um, okay."

"Seems like it's our karma to travel awhile together in this lifetime," she continued as we approached the parking lot entrance. "We both love your dad, and he and I have been soul mates over many lifetimes. Can't you and I get along?"

By this time, I was ready to leap from the moving car like James Bond. "Sure, whatever," I mumbled. The instant we stopped, I flung the door open.

"Just call us when you're done," said Shasta. "Have fun!"

Hopping out, I muttered something in reply. This woman only complicated things when she spoke the truth and acted vulnerable and stuff. Why couldn't she just keep quiet and play the wicked stepmother?

I joined the flow of kids headed for the Rangers meeting. Up ahead, Kelvin Chang was chatting with Hulk Jr., and Zit Face was stealing glances at the three girls, who walked in a cluster like girls do.

"Wait up, chamaco!" came a voice from behind.

Nacho trotted up to join me.

"Well, if it isn't Prisoner One-Nine-Two-Two," I said. "How're things in lockup?"

"No jailbreaks, no knife fights; it's just capital-B boring," he said, in an old-timey gangster voice. "You?"

"The same."

We drifted toward the picnic tables while catching up. I couldn't put my finger on it, but something at the meeting seemed a little different today. Brayden, the redheaded kid, was throwing his pocketknife, same as last time. Kelvin the Pyro was playing with a Zippo lighter. But the overall mood seemed more low-key somehow.

And then I realized why. Mr. Papadakis, the troop sponsor, was there. A big olive-skinned guy with curly salt-and-pepper hair, he looked like a football linebacker who'd won more than his share of hot dog eating contests.

"Everyone, please take a seat," he said, beckoning us forward. When the troop had settled, he said, "For those of you who don't know me, I'm Joe Papadakis of Big Papa Sports, which sponsors your troop." A smattering of applause followed this.

Mr. Papadakis held up a hand in acknowledgment and continued. "You don't usually see much of me, but I'm here today because we've got some changes happening in Troop Nineteen."

Nacho nudged me. "Hey, where's Brozny?"

I scanned the area. The walrus-shaped man was nowhere to be seen, but a tall stranger hovered on the edge of the group.

"As you may have noticed, Mr. Brozny isn't with us anymore," said Mr. Papadakis.

"Where'd he go?" asked Bridget.

Frankie's smile was wry. "Couldn't handle girls in his troop?"

"Mr. Brozny has, uh, moved on to pursue other opportunities," said our troop sponsor.

"He quit," whispered Nacho.

"Or was fired," I said.

The big man spread his arms. "We wish him well,

but now I want you to help me welcome your new troopmaster."

The tall stranger strode forward like a sword blade slicing the air. His every move said, *Don't mess with me, sweet cheeks.*

"Who the heck is *that?*" I asked.

6

Hard Corps

"This," said Mr. Papadakis, "is an old friend of mine from the Corps. Rangers, please welcome retired Marine Corps captain Rockwell Hamilton Pierce."

Dutiful applause greeted this announcement. Most of us were too busy getting our heads around the idea of having a new troopmaster to give him a proper welcome.

Mr. Pierce moved like a panther, if a panther had had a yardstick glued to its back. His walnut-brown skin gleamed in the sunshine, his lean body looked tougher than rhino gristle, and a frown had carved two deep grooves in his forehead. Incredibly, he made the dorky Rangers uniform look like it came from some elite new military branch. Instead of the goofy cap we wore, he sported a Canadian Mounties–type hat with a flat, broad brim.

Our new leader waited until the whispers had

quieted. With legs apart and hands behind his back, he stood like a general reviewing his troops.

"Thank you, Rangers," he said. "And thank you, Sergeant." Mr. Pierce nodded at the store owner.

"*Semper fi,*" said Mr. Papadakis, shaking a fist.

I glanced over at Nacho for a translation.

"Don't look at me," he whispered. "That's not Spanish."

"For twelve years," said Mr. Pierce, "I molded mere grunts into members of the world's most elite fighting force."

"The Avengers?" I whispered.

Nacho bit a knuckle to keep from laughing.

"The US Marines," continued our new troopmaster, who luckily hadn't overheard me. "And I look forward to the challenge of molding you young men and women into Rangers."

Zit Face's hand shot up. "Uh, sir?"

Mr. Pierce's eagle eyes raked over Zit Face. "Yes, Mister . . . ?"

"Burns," said Zit Face, his voice cracking. "Nate Burns."

"Fire away."

Nate's big Adam's apple bobbed up and down. "Did you see any, uh . . . action in the Marine Corps?"

Mr. Pierce considered the question. "I had the privilege of serving this country in Iraq and Afghanistan. And I don't mind telling you, things got pretty hot over there. My unit was in the sh—" Glancing over at Mr. Papadakis, he seemed to reconsider. "The, er, thick of the action. We lost some brave men and women."

"Yeah, but did you kill anybody?" I asked. I knew the question sounded bratty as soon as it left my mouth, but all this *Sample Fly* business was rubbing me the wrong way.

Those sharp eyes turned on me. "Why do you ask, Mister . . . ?"

"Coop, uh, Cooper McCall." I shrugged. "Just curious."

His fierce gaze held mine, and I felt like an impala being sized up for a lion's lunch. But when Mr. Pierce spoke, his voice was softer. "Yes, I did."

An "oooh" rippled through the group.

The ex-Marine didn't seem to hear. A shadow passed over his face and he looked like he was watching something far, far away. "Death comes to us all, soon or late. What matters is how we react. Will you whimper and hide, or will you face it like a warrior?"

A chill trickled down my spine. Dang, this guy leading the Boy Rangers was like Thor using his hammer to build birdhouses. Overkill? Oh, just a little.

At the next table, I noticed Frankie nodding and frowning in sympathy. Most of the other Rangers looked a little confused. They'd expected to earn achievement badges in Pathfinding and Fire Safety, not Dying Bravely on the Battlefield.

Was this guy planning to turn us into soldiers?

Mr. Papadakis must have read the group's confusion. He stepped forward, clapping Captain Cheerful on the shoulder.

"I'm sure you're all going to get along just fine. I'll leave you now to get acquainted with your new leader, but feel free to call me with any questions." He snapped off a salute to Mr. Pierce. "Captain."

The ex-Marine returned it. "Sergeant."

The big store owner lumbered off, leaving us all alone with the lean, green killing machine. For an uncomfortably long time, the troopmaster surveyed us with a fierce squint that would've made Jack the Ripper cry "Mommy!"

"Let's see what you're made of," he said, almost to himself. Then, in a voice like a bullwhip crack, Mr. Pierce belted out, "Troop, fall in!"

Everyone flinched, then looked at each other for a clue. Nothing but shrugs and puzzled faces.

"Fall in what?" I asked.

The squint got squintier. The ex-Marine stalked up to me with his ramrod panther gait. *"Sir,"* he said.

"How's that?"

"When you address me, you will address me as 'sir' or 'troopmaster,'" he said, looming over me. His citrusy aftershave was strong enough to beat The Rock in arm wrestling. Pierce's gaze took in the rest of the Rangers.

"When you're here, I am the source of all authority," he continued. "The outside world does not exist. I am your mother, your father, your priest, your principal, your private deity. If I say *jump*, you say, *how high?*"

We all stared at him like he'd lost his mind.

"Understood?" Mr. Pierce snapped.

"Um, yeah," I muttered, and most of the group followed suit. Only Bridget said, "Yes, sir."

"What's that?" Mr. Pierce yelled.

"Yes, sir," we said, more or less together.

A muscle jumped in the troopmaster's jaw. "Speak up, microbes. I can't hear you!"

Microbes?

"Yes, *sir*!" we shouted. Although I only said it because he was standing right in front of me.

Mr. Pierce nodded. "When you fall in, it means you line up in rows, standing at attention. Can you do that, you worthless pig ticklers?"

I started to say "Yeah," but his glare turned it into a "Yes, sir!" like everyone else's.

"Line up on that lawn at my command," said the troopmaster. "Troop . . . fall in!"

At a normal pace, we stood and began to shuffle over to the spot he'd indicated.

"No lollygagging!" Mr. Pierce bellowed. "Quick-time!"

"Jeez, what's up with Commander Crankypants?" I mumbled to Nacho as we hurried onto the grass.

"His parents potty trained him too early?" Nacho guessed.

Forming up in three raggedy rows, we stared at our new leader with suspicion. Brozny was useless, sure, but this guy? Even my mom would have to agree, this level of discipline was overkill. I didn't know what Rangers was supposed to be like, but surely it wasn't supposed to be like *this*.

Mr. Pierce paced down the front line, glaring. "This is, without a doubt, the laziest, sloppiest unit I have ever come across. Do none of you bug smugglers know how to stand at attention?"

Shrugs and headshakes answered his question. But surprisingly, one person responded. Chubby José, one of the least military-looking kids around, straightened his spine, threw back his shoulders, and clicked his heels together.

Troopmaster Pierce nodded. "That's how we do it. Troop, atten . . . *hut!*"

Heels clicked, backs straightened, and we all managed to look a bit more like José. But that wasn't enough for Mr. Pierce. Not nearly enough. Over and over, he drilled us—fall in, fall out, parade rest, attention, quick-march—trotting us around the field like disobedient pups at a dog show.

Only near the very end of the meeting did he ask us to demonstrate a few Ranger-type things—knot tying, using a compass, and so forth. Finally, the troopmaster had us fall in once more, standing at attention in the afternoon sun. By this time, I was hot, tired, sweaty, and in no mood to play soldier.

Once again, Mr. Pierce gave us a long stare before speaking. "Disgraceful!" he said at last. "You pathetic cheesemongers can barely follow drill commands, most of you are out of shape, and no one here seems to know a compass from a cuckoo clock."

I couldn't take it anymore. Hot words bubbled up and out of my mouth. "Maybe that's because half of us just joined last weekend, and nobody ever showed us any of this stuff before." When the troopmaster's glare seemed about to burn a hole in my face, I added, "Sir."

For a long beat, he just stared. Then he glanced over at Bridget, standing tall in the front row. "Is this true?"

"Yes, sir!" she barked.

"Well, then," said Mr. Pierce. "You all have a lot to learn if I'm going to turn you from the rancid fridge biscuits that you are into real live Rangers. I can see I've got my work cut out for me. Troop, fall out!"

On the phone with Mom that night, I tried to appeal

to her sympathetic side. "Please? I've learned my lesson. Can I *please* quit the Rangers?"

She chuckled. "Aw, what's wrong, honey boy? Did you try this on your dad and he didn't listen?"

"That's not the issue," I said. "The Rangers are terrible."

"You know what else is terrible?" Mom said. "Trespassing at a theme park." In the background, I could hear the TV playing.

Pacing up and down in Dad's office, I said, "You don't understand. This new troopmaster is driving me crazy."

"He can't be that bad."

"He is! He makes us march around like soldiers."

"Uh-huh," said Mom.

I waved my free hand about. "He—he insults us left and right, and we have to exercise like mad."

"I see."

"And we always have to say 'yes, sir' and 'no, sir.' I hate it."

"Sounds perfect," said my mom.

My jaw dropped. "Have you not heard a single thing I'm saying?"

"Every word." The TV noise muted behind her. "Honey, you need to learn discipline. And from what you say, discipline is exactly what this man is delivering."

"But—"

"I'm so grateful, I should go up and give Mr. Pierce a big ol' kiss."

My skin crawled. "Eeeww, gross."

She chuckled again. "Sorry, but you're staying in the Rangers."

"You are so mean," I huffed, slumping into the sofa cushions.

"The meanest mom around," she said. "Sleep well, honey boy. I'll see you tomorrow afternoon."

7

Noodle Arms

In my third week of being grounded, I was so stir-crazy I almost welcomed the change of pace that the Rangers meetings provided.

Almost.

A guy has his limits, after all.

On Tuesday, as we hung out by the picnic tables, waiting for Troopmaster Pierce, Nacho was busy chatting with Tavia and Hulk Jr., whose name turned out to be Xander. So I eased up next to Frankie Patel.

"What do you think of our new leader?"

She folded forward over one leg, stretching out her hamstring. "He's . . . different, that's for sure."

"Yeah, but he shouldn't rag on us like that."

"Aw, it's not so bad," said Frankie.

"Really?" I rested a fist on my hip. "Calling us lazy

and disgraceful? Microbes and cheesemongers? What kind of grown-up abuses kids that way?"

"Um, a coach?" Frankie glanced up at me as she switched legs.

I looked away so she wouldn't think I'd been noticing her legs in those shorts. "Come on."

She bent forward again. "Seriously. My AYSO coach last year was twice as bad."

"Then why not just bail?"

Frankie glanced at me sidelong. "It's not necessarily a bad thing."

"Getting insulted?"

She shook her head. "They only do it to help us improve. It's, like, tough love."

I snorted. "Yeah? How did you get to know so much?"

"Mine is an ancient culture," said Frankie. "I was born with natural wisdom."

I swatted her with my cap.

Just then, a deep voice from behind us boomed, "Troop, fall in!" And in a flash, Mr. Pierce was back.

This time, though, it wasn't enough that we stood at attention. No, he wanted us evenly spaced out. So we had to "dress right," which meant extending our left arms to touch the shoulder of the person beside us. (Shouldn't they have called it "dress left"?)

Once we were arranged to his satisfaction, the troop-master spoke. "After last week's disastrous showing, I did some serious thinking."

"Me too," I whispered to Nacho.

He fought to keep a straight face. We were standing in the back row, so I felt fairly safe making comments.

"Not to criticize your last troopmaster, but this unit is in terrible shape," said Mr. Pierce.

"Criticize him, criticize him," whispered Nacho. And now it was my turn to bite my lip.

Mr. Pierce paced in front of us, *tap-tap-tapping* a riding crop against his leg. That was new. And disturbing. "You prune-faced dogburgers lack discipline, lack skills, and worst of all, lack esprit de corps."

"What's spree decor?" I muttered. "Some new style of home design?"

Nacho snorted.

Mr. Pierce's laser gaze locked in on me. "McCall."

Dang. The guy had ears like a German shepherd. "Yes, um, sir?"

"Drop and give me twenty."

"What? You gotta be kidding."

When I didn't instantly hop to it, he snapped, "Now, Ranger!"

"All right, all right," I grumbled.

Face burning, I got down into push-up position and began slowly pumping them out. One . . . two . . . three . . .

I couldn't see Mr. Pierce's face just then, but I was pretty sure he was glaring at my fellow Rangers when he said, "Since your last leader didn't lay down the law, I will. Smart comments, interruptions, and disrespect will not be tolerated. If you have a question, you ask my permission first. Understood?"

"Yes, sir." Their response was raggedy.

"I can't hear you," snapped the troopmaster.

"Yes, sir!"

Somewhere around twelve or thirteen push-ups, my arms got shaky. I wasn't weak, you understand. Just out of practice. I seriously hoped Frankie wasn't watching.

"Eighteen . . ." I panted.

"Thirteen," Mr. Pierce corrected me, then continued. "I've decided that Troop Nineteen needs a goal, some kind of worthy challenge to build your team spirit."

Bridget Click must have raised her hand, because the troopmaster said, "Yes, Miss Click."

"Do you mean like a fundraiser?" she asked, adding "Sir?" for good measure.

Tap-tap-tap went the riding crop against his leg. "No, I'm talking about a contest, something that will push you to your limits."

"Ooh." Her eyes lit up.

Speaking of limits, I'd just about hit mine. My

chest ached, my face was on fire, and my arms trembled like saplings in a hurricane. I took a short break with my chest on the ground. Just to catch my breath.

"This troop is going to enter the Wilderness Jamboree," said Mr. Pierce.

"Woo-hoo!" cried Bridget.

"What's that?" somebody asked. "Um, sir."

Suddenly, a face loomed just above me. "Taking a nap, you miserable worm smoocher?"

"Counting grass blades," I said.

The troopmaster's eyes narrowed. "You think you're funny, but you're not. You're just a microorganism that crawled out of some elephant puke."

Elephant puke? Microorganism? Was this guy watching too much Nature Channel or what?

"Put some oomph into it!"

Glowering at his boots, I managed to pump out another push-up.

"Seventeen," said Mr. Pierce.

My arms wobbled uncontrollably, but I pulled off one more.

"Eighteen." A couple of the Rangers standing near me had joined in the count.

My face flamed from embarrassment, and my body

buckled and jerked like an inchworm having a fit. But somehow I forced myself up.

"Nnnnineteen."

From the down position, I pushed, but nothing happened. I pushed again.

Nothing.

This brought to mind every snotty PE coach, every gym class humiliation I'd ever suffered.

"Push, Ranger!" snapped Mr. Pierce.

"I . . . am . . . pushing," I grunted out between clenched teeth.

My chest and arms were pure, pulsating pain. But no matter how hard I strained, I couldn't lift my body more than a couple of inches before it collapsed. And that was that. I couldn't have done any more push-ups for love or money.

"Appalling. All right, McCall. *Atten . . . hut!*"

My arms had zero strength left. I had to flop over onto my back and sit up before I could cross my legs and stand. Nacho sent me a sympathetic wince.

Mr. Pierce surveyed the group. "Now, do we all understand the rules?"

"Yes, sir!" came the answer.

He nodded, satisfied for the moment. "The Wilderness Jamboree, for those who don't know, is the annual competition for Rangers. Troops come from all over the country to test their Ranger skills against each other."

Tavia raised her hand. "We're going to visit the Jamboree, sir?"

"We're going to *win* the Jamboree, Ranger," said Mr. Pierce, leveling a steely gaze on the troop.

And then I couldn't help it. I burst out laughing.

8

Dinner and a Spat

As I'd expected, Mr. Pierce had zero sense of humor. Since my arms had already turned to soba noodles from all the push-ups, he made me run laps for my rudeness.

Then, before we quit for the day, he explained a bit more about the Wilderness Jamboree. Not just any troop could attend. All members had to earn a minimum number of achievement badges first, to prove our abilities.

"Is there a limit to how many badges we can get?" asked Bridget.

Mr. Pierce consulted his information sheet. "None. But everyone has to at least achieve the basics— Pathfinding, Fire Safety, Knot Tying, Camping, and so forth."

Bridget smiled a private smile. I suspected she planned to be the first Ranger in history to earn *all* the badges before Jamboree, even Parasailing, Dentistry, and Nuclear Science. It sounded like a lot of work to me.

"And that's not all," Pierce continued. *Oh, great.* "You cake-eating snot goblins also must complete a special activity to qualify—but more about that next time."

Bridget and José were the only ones who groaned in disappointment. The rest of us gaped, still a bit stunned.

As Nacho and I trudged home, he turned to me. "I never thought I'd be saying this."

"What?"

"I miss Brozny."

"Me too."

Only a couple of weeks into it, and I had to face the facts. So far, Mom and Dad's Summer of Discipline was winning out over my Summer of Getting Them Back Together. As soon as I returned home from our dismal Rangers meeting, I resolved to do something about that.

Soothing my wounded pride with a Fudgsicle, I flopped onto the couch to plot and plan. After some hard thinking (and a couple more Fudgsicles), I realized several things:

1. Getting my folks back together meant that I first needed to keep them happy.

2. Keeping them happy meant that I'd probably have to stay in the Rangers, at least for the time being. (*Ugh.* The sacrifices I make.)

3. Mom and Dad needed reminders of how good it used to be when they were together.

4. That meant tricking them into doing things that they used to like doing together.

I scratched my head, thinking back to my parents' activities when they weren't arguing all the time. Cleaning the house? Nah. Watching their favorite TV show? Uh-uh.

An image from long ago popped into my mind. Mom and Dad getting dressed up for dinner out, laughing and smooching each other, while I groused about staying home with a babysitter.

Dinner out.

Hmmm . . .

It just might work, but only if I took them by surprise. Mom still hadn't returned my cell phone, so I called Dad from the landline. When he picked up, I said, "Hey, I want to take you out to dinner."

"What brought this on?" he asked.

"Oh, I just feel bad."

"You're sick?"

"No," I said, curling the ancient phone cord around my finger. "I, um, feel bad about all the trouble I've caused lately. I want to make it up to you."

Squeals and giggles sounded in the background. "That's, uh, that's nice of you. Put that down."

"Excuse me?"

"Not you," said Dad. "Piper, sweetie, that's enough."

"Dad?"

"Yeah, buddy," he said. "I'll see you Friday. Why don't we have dinner then?"

By this time, my finger was fully wrapped up in the curly phone cord like a mummy in linen. I tried to pull it free. "No, please. I'd really like to do something special."

"Well . . ."

"Dinner at Cyrano's?" I said. "Tomorrow night?"

Cyrano's Bistro was his and Mom's favorite

restaurant. I couldn't count how many times they'd told me the story of their first date there, and how he was so nervous he forgot to bring his wallet, and blah, blah, blah. Typical parent stuff.

But it meant something to them.

Dad said, "I don't know . . ."

"Please, Dad?" I played the guilt card. "You didn't have time for our hike last weekend, and I'd really like some special time with you."

"Well . . . it's not our usual night," he said. "But I guess if it's okay with your mother . . ."

"It totally is!" (It totally wasn't. She had no idea.)

Finally, he caved, we set a time, and I told him Mom would drop me off there.

One down.

Next, I approached Mom, who was preparing some chicken katsu, Japanese-style fried chicken, for dinner. When I gave her the same invitation, a little smile played across her lips.

"Cyrano's?" she said, and her eyes got a soft, far-off look.

"Yeah," I said. "Just you and me. I want to show you how sorry I am."

Her eyebrows lifted. "And where will you get the money for this fancy dinner?"

"My piggy bank." It'd been ages since I tapped that old-fashioned bank Nana C had given me a couple of Christmases ago. "It's stuffed to the brim."

After a bit more urging, she agreed. Now I had both parents lined up. All I had to do was walk them down memory lane over some fancy risotto, and abracadabra! Back together again. When a bubble of guilt welled up at the thought of what this would do to Shasta's girls, I squashed it back down in a heartbeat.

My plan was perfect.

My plan couldn't miss.

The first hitch came late Wednesday afternoon, when I went to raid my piggy bank. Pulling the rubber plug from the pig's belly, I shook the bank. Out dropped two crumpled ten-dollar bills and a bunch of quarters.

I shook the piggy bank harder, and a five-dollar bill joined the pile.

That's all?

Probing inside with a pencil, I managed to locate another three singles. And that was that. I groaned. Maybe I'd broken into the piggy bank for the last video game I'd bought, but surely I hadn't spent that much?

I considered my stash. Thirty-one dollars and fifty cents, all told.

Hmm. Would that be enough? It had to be.

Future Coop would deal with the financing problem. Present Coop needed to finish getting ready.

All dressed up in my nicest shirt and slacks, my maybe-not-enough money stuffed in one pocket, I hopped into Mom's old blue Prius and off we went. The second hitch came when we reached the restaurant.

I'd hoped that we'd beat my dad there, so that he'd walk in, see the both of us in his favorite restaurant, and get all gooey and sentimental. Instead, he pulled into the parking lot just as we were crossing to the entrance.

"Mari?" he said through the open window. "I didn't know you'd be joining us."

She gave me a searching look. "Neither did I."

"Well, I should leave you guys to—" he began.

I jumped in. "Hey, I never get the chance to have dinner with both my favorite people anymore."

"Cooper . . ." Mom said.

"Mom, we're all here," I said. "You both made time for it. Please let me treat you to show how sorry I am?"

Mom and Dad exchanged a look.

After a long pause, Dad lifted a shoulder. "I guess."

It wasn't enthusiastic, but it would have to do.

"Great," I said. "Let's all go inside."

The waitress led us to our table, which had a real candle and a vase with a red flower in it. I smiled to myself. *Can't beat flowers and candles for setting the mood,* I thought. Passing the waitress fifty cents as a tip, I said, "Thanks for making it romantic."

She gave me a baffled look and hurried off to seat another party. But I knew, deep down, she appreciated my thoughtfulness.

The third hitch came when I opened the menu. *Twenty-five dollars for risotto? Yeesh! Was it gold-plated or had it been hand-cooked by a Roman emperor?* With these prices, I'd be lucky if I could treat *one* of my parents.

"What's wrong?" asked Mom.

"Nothing," I said. "I'm, uh, just . . . not as hungry as I thought."

My dad's eyebrow lifted. "Really?"

"Yeah, you guys get what you like. I'll stick with the bread."

As soon as the words left my lips, I felt it sounded suspicious. Everyone knew I was a charter member of the Clean Plate Club, and never *ever* turned down food.

Both parents stared. Mom placed the back of her hand on my forehead.

"Really," I said. "I'm fine."

We went ahead and ordered. Surveying the place, I took in the white tablecloths, the dim lighting, and the faint jazzy music. Perfect. I scrutinized my parents, waiting for the magic to happen.

Mom shifted in her chair like she couldn't get comfortable. Dad checked his phone as a text buzzed in, probably from Shasta McNasty. I frowned. Maybe my parents needed a nudge.

"So, I guess this place really brings back memories, huh?" I said.

Mom's eyes flicked to Dad's face and away. Glancing up from his phone, Dad said, "Memories. Yeah."

She tore her slice of bread in half, then in half again.

"That's such a great story, the one about your first date here," I said. "I'd love to hear it again?"

"Maybe some other time," said my mom.

Putting down his phone, Dad focused on me. "So, how's that new troopmaster working out?"

I grimaced. This wasn't supposed to be their discussion topic.

"Uh, okay, I guess," I said. "Hey, what was your favorite dish when you guys used to come here on dates?"

Dad didn't take the bait. "Coop, what's wrong with the new guy?"

"He's, uh, pretty strict," I said.

Dad grunted. "That's good. Strict rules will help you learn discipline."

"But he made Coop do push-ups until his arms gave out," said my mom. "That seems kind of extreme."

A frown creased Dad's forehead. "Why did he make you do that?"

I stared down at my bread. "No reason."

"Cooper?"

"He didn't like how I was talking to him," I mumbled.

Dad's voice took on an edge. "You sassed the man? I'd say push-ups is a fair punishment."

"Coop could've torn a muscle," said my mom, her tone matching his. "It's excessive."

Dad's face flushed. "It's no more than any coach would've done."

"Oh, really?"

"You always want to coddle the boy."

"And you always want to throw the book at him," said my mom.

My gut wound tighter than a superhero's spandex. This *really* wasn't going the way I'd planned.

Even the waitress arriving with our food didn't stop their squabbling. Despite my best efforts, Mom and Dad bickered all the way through to their dessert, a chocolate mousse that I *really* wanted for myself. No matter how I tried steering the conversation back to happier days, they seemed determined to fight. Finally the check arrived.

"I've got it," I said miserably.

And then I saw the total.

My eyes practically popped out like Bugs Bunny's when he drinks hot sauce. *Sixty-nine dollars?* For two meals? How was that even possible?

Emptying my pocket, I piled all my money onto the bill, every last quarter. As our waitress served a nearby table, I waved at her to see if she'd give me back my fifty-cent tip, but she didn't notice. Mom craned her neck to read the bill.

"Need a little help there?" she said.

"Uh . . . maybe?" Unless I wanted to wash dishes at Cyrano's for the next two months.

Reaching over, Dad snatched the check and cash. "I've got it."

"No, let me," said Mom, making a grab.

After another brief squabble over who would pay, my dad finally plunked down his credit card. Shooting me a direct look from under his shaggy eyebrows, he said, "Looks like someone still has a few things to learn about responsibility."

I slumped lower in my seat. What could you say to that?

He was right. If I was responsible for getting my parents back together, I'd just had an epic fail.

9

Poodle vs. Moose

Three Rangers meetings per week was three meetings too many, in my opinion. But nobody asked my opinion. The night of our disastrous family dinner, Mr. Pierce sent out an email to all the parents, trying to psych them up about the Jamboree. He encouraged them to support their kids and help us get "competition-ready."

The other Rangers' parents were overjoyed, I'm sure. One more goal for their kids to achieve. Nacho and I held a different opinion.

This guy is the worst, he texted me a couple of hours before Thursday's meeting. (We'd gotten our phones back—at last.)

Me: Agreed. Major suckage. ☹

Nacho: Any luck getting out of rangers?

Me: Nope. U still grounded?

Nacho: Until Saturday. U?

Me: Same.

Nacho: We need 2 teach pierce a lesson!!!

Me: Hmmm. I'll think of something.

Nacho: Something big.

Me: Ok, chamaco.

Nacho: Later, chamaco.

Although Mom had approved of my joining the Rangers, she still had her doubts about Mr. Pierce. So when she dropped me at the school that day, she turned off the car and opened her door.

"Where are you going?" I said.

"I want to meet this Mr. Pierce."

I held up my palms. "Whoa. Totally not necessary."

"It's not for you," she said, "it's for me."

"You don't even have to do it for *you*," I said.

But Mom had her game face on. I knew from past experience that my arguments wouldn't work when she was like this. Did that stop me? No way. I gave it another shot before surrendering. But the outcome was never in doubt.

"Okay," I said at last. "Do your thing."

Who knows? Maybe she'd take him down a notch or two. Ooh—or maybe she'd even get mad enough to yank me out of Rangers.

I let her pull ahead of me as we crossed the lot to join the others. Nacho drifted up. "Ay, chamaco, you brought your mom?"

"She brought me."

He grimaced. "Still . . ."

"You ever tried to stop one of your moms from doing something?" I asked.

"Good point," he said.

By the time we reached the picnic tables, my mother was right up in Mr. Pierce's face. It was almost funny, seeing this tiny woman going after a tall guy, like a teacup poodle attacking a moose.

I hesitated, torn. On the one hand, I didn't want to be anywhere near that action. But on the other hand, that action was all about me. Casually, I drifted toward the picnic table closest to them, where Bridget

Click was showing Xander and Tavia something in the Ranger Handbook.

"Ma'am, you don't understand," the troopmaster was telling my mom. "I've been training men and women for over a decade. I—"

"Ma'am?" she said. "I'm no ma'am; I'm younger than you are."

"Ooh, shots fired," said Nacho in my ear. "The moms don't like the 'ma'am.'"

I stifled a snort.

Pierce waved away my mom's comment. "Regardless. I know what works. I know what I'm doing."

Mom's fists found their way to her hips. "Do you? Did it ever occur to you that these are boys and girls, not men and women?"

"Of course. These kids' parents want them to learn wilderness skills and discipline. That's what I deliver."

"Your methods are extreme."

"My methods work."

For a long, long moment, they glared at each other. I couldn't be sure, but it almost seemed like they were on the verge of cracking up.

Weird.

The troopmaster cut his eyes toward us. "I've got a meeting to run."

"And I've got places to go," Mom said, still holding his gaze.

"Maybe we could continue this another time?"

A corner of Mom's mouth pulled up. "Over dinner?"

Mr. Pierce's grim mouth curled in an answering smile. "I'll call. Your number's on the troop roster."

My mouth dropped open. When I turned to Nacho to say, *Did you see that?*, his jaw had fallen open too. We must have looked like two baby birds at feeding time.

"Oooh!" Bridget's sharp elbow dug into my ribs. "Looks like someone's mom has a crush on our troopmaster."

"Shut up," I said. "She does not."

But before we could get into it, Mr. Pierce called, "Troop . . . fall in!"

We lined up, and for a few heartbeats, our troopmaster just stared at us. Then without warning, he barked, "Who's the best troop?"

After exchanging puzzled glances, most of us stayed quiet. Bridget raised a tentative hand. "Um, I've heard Troop Eleven in Monterrosa is pretty good."

"No," said Mr. Pierce, with a challenging look. "*Who's* the best troop?"

Most of us just shrugged.

"You're missing the point," he said. "*You're* the best troop."

A laugh popped out before I could stop it. "Excuse me? We can't even read a compass. Um, sir."

Hands behind his back, Mr. Pierce strutted along our formation. "Excellence begins with belief. If you don't *believe* you're the best, how can you expect to *be* the best?"

"We can't?" said Frankie.

"Precisely. So I'll ask you again, you lily-livered scum guzzlers. Who's the best troop?"

"We are?" said José and Tavia.

"And what's your troop number, Rangers?" barked Mr. Pierce.

"Troop Nineteen." This time, a few other kids joined them.

Cupping a hand to his ear, the ex-Marine singsonged, "I can't *hear* you, microbes. Who's the best troop?"

"Troop Nineteen!"

He had us repeat it until we were yelling at the top of our lungs. But I have to say, I didn't believe it any more the fifth time than I did the first.

We still had a *long* way to go.

As we Rangers stood sweating in the hot sun, our troopmaster laid out his plan for the eight and a half weeks left before the Wilderness Jamboree. It was, in a word, bazonkers.

But though I listened to his announcement, only one thought occupied my mind: *My mom wants to go out with this guy?*

Seriously. I mean, this maniac expected us to learn everything from archery, astronomy, and Morse code to fishing, first aid, and wilderness survival—and in just eight-plus weeks. I glanced over to Nacho and he rolled his eyes. I agreed. No way could we learn all that so fast.

Bridget Click, on the other hand, looked like she was soaring up to heaven on golden wings. With each new skill he mentioned, her smile grew. Little Miss Overachiever.

"Mr. Pierce, sir, may I just say how pleased I am that you're letting us compete in the Jamboree? Mr. Brozny wouldn't even consider it."

A sardonic smile twisted our leader's lips. "I'm not Mr. Brozny."

Understatement of the year.

"Now, I know you Rangers are curious about the special qualifying activity I mentioned last time," said Mr. Pierce.

"Yes, sir!" said Bridget, José, and Nate.

"Just under three weeks from now, we will take an overnight camping trip," said Mr. Pierce. "Perform well, and we go to the Jamboree." He glared at us. "Performing poorly is not an option."

"Camping?" said Nacho, forgetting to raise his hand. "Like, in nature?"

The troopmaster's steely gray eyes almost twinkled. "That's usually where you camp, Ranger."

Bridget's hand shot up. "Mr. Pierce, sir?" When he nodded at her, she said, "He forgot to say sir, sir."

"Thank you, Miss Click. I'm aware." To my eye, it

looked like he wasn't pushing the matter because he was enjoying my friend's discomfort.

Nacho gulped. As I knew very well, his idea of roughing it was riding his bike to the video arcade instead of being dropped off. I was no Bear Grylls myself, but at least I'd been on nature walks with my dad.

This campout would be *interesting.*

After dumping the plan on us (without asking for our input), Mr. Pierce thwacked his riding crop against his leg and announced, "Physical conditioning is a key element of success at the Jamboree. That means we'll spend the first half hour of each meeting between now and then by whipping you lazy, phone-obsessed booger farmers into shape. You will run, you will do push-ups, and you will love it!"

"In your dreams," I muttered to Kelvin.

Mr. Pierce must've had ears like a bat. "McCall!"

"Yes . . . sir?"

"Thanks for volunteering." His smile had a sharky edge to it.

I blinked. "Excuse me?"

"Wasn't that you I heard, volunteering to show everyone proper running form?"

Glancing at my fellow Rangers for help, I said, "No, I—"

"Splendid." The troopmaster pointed at the far

fence that bounded the athletic field. "Take a couple laps around the perimeter and show us how it's done."

"But that's not—" I began.

"Now, Ranger!" he barked. "That's an order."

"You're not the boss of me," I said.

Mr. Pierce looked almost amused. "Actually, I am. At least while the Rangers are meeting. I'm the next best thing to God."

"But—"

"And you will address me as 'sir.'"

I started to object further, but then I remembered the push-ups fiasco. "Okay . . . sir." Heaving a massive sigh, I started jogging toward the far fence.

"Faster!" yelled the ex-Marine. "Pick up the pace!"

I picked up the pace. I was running, all right. But contrary to what he'd promised, I wasn't loving it.

Hot, sweaty, and red-faced, we all gathered around the picnic tables after Pierce tired of torturing us. Frankie and Tavia, the soccer players, were barely winded. I resolved to change my mind about the benefits of organized sports.

Mr. Pierce handed out compasses and placed a stack of maps on a picnic table.

"Pathfinding is one of the cornerstones of wilderness

survival," he said. "If you couldn't read your map and compass, where would you be?"

"Um, checking your phone's GPS?" said Kelvin.

The ex-Marine shot him a withering look. "But what if you're out of cell range? Or your phone's battery dies. What then, Chang?"

Kelvin lifted a shoulder. "You'd be lost?"

"Precisely. Gather round."

Forming a half circle around him, we watched as Mr. Pierce demonstrated how to orient the topographic map, making sure to align the compass edge with the map's north-south meridians. It looked easy enough. He pointed out several landmarks—the Mayor's Hill, the old church, and so forth—comparing their map positions to where they stood in real life.

"That's how you check that you're properly oriented," he said. "Make sense?"

"Yes, sir."

Then it was our turn. First, we broke into teams of two and took turns orienting the map. Simple enough. After that, Pierce had us follow a series of easy instructions ("Take five steps south, then ten steps west") that led us around the school grounds.

All five teams passed with flying colors. I have

to admit, even though I didn't want to be there, it still gave me a warm glow to be mastering a new skill. Nacho, however, looked like he'd been force-fed a plate of soggy broccoli.

"All right, you knock-kneed ninnyhammers," Mr. Pierce barked. "One final test, and you'll have earned your Pathfinding achievement badge."

Bridget clapped her hands together. I rolled my eyes.

Passing out a slip of paper to each team, our leader said, "I've placed five orange traffic cones in five locations, with a prize under each cone. Your challenge: Follow these instructions, claim your prize, and return here by fifteen-hundred hours."

"That's an awful lot of time for a simple exercise, sir," said Brayden, scratching his head. "Isn't that something like sixty days?"

Pierce briefly shut his eyes. "Military clock, Ranger. Fifteen-hundred means three o'clock. Comprende?"

The redhead blushed. "Yessir," he mumbled.

"Any other questions?" Nobody spoke. Probably no one else wanted to expose their ignorance. "Then start pathfinding. Troop . . . dismissed!"

Claiming a picnic table for ourselves, Nacho and I reviewed the instructions.

"Piece of cake," I said. "Most of it is just a straight line to the southwest."

"If it takes us away from here," said Nacho, "I'm all for it."

Compasses out, we followed the bearing. It

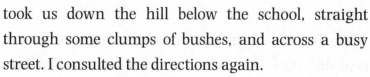

took us down the hill below the school, straight through some clumps of bushes, and across a busy street. I consulted the directions again.

"Now we head east for—"

"Hold up," said Nacho. His eyebrow arched. He gave me That Look. "You know what's just a little ways to the west, don't you?"

I glanced down the road.

"The arcade," we said together.

Feeling a grin tugging at the corners of my mouth, I said, "I don't think the Rangers would mind if we took a *little* detour."

"Then what are we waiting for?"

10

Arcade Hero

After the heat of the day, the air-conditioned arcade provided cool (and noisy) relief. Quarters dropped, video games dinged and chimed, and all was right with the world.

"Ahh," said Nacho. "Home, sweet home."

"Just what the doctor ordered," I agreed.

We played a few rounds of Guitar Hero and Zelda, laughing at the thought of the other Rangers stumbling around town, sweating it up. *Suckers.* This was more like the summer I'd had in mind.

But all too soon, our money ran out. I cast a wistful glance at Guitar Hero. "Guess we should be getting back."

Nacho heaved a sigh. "Too bad they won't let us play on credit."

It wasn't until we were tromping down the main road that I realized we wouldn't make it back in time— particularly if we stopped to collect the prize in Pierce's orange cone.

"So?" said Nacho. "We'll just tell him that someone stole it."

"Works for me."

A niggling doubt suggested we were letting the troop down, but I quickly smothered it.

We'd almost reached the spot where we'd entered the road before. I nodded at a white-haired old lady coming down her front steps, and we turned to cross the street.

"Aagh!"

A sudden cry spun us both around. The woman lay crumpled like an abandoned candy wrapper on her front walk.

Rushing to her side, I knelt down. "Are you all right?"

When she looked up, a trickle of blood ran down

her forehead. "Huh?" the woman slurred, her eyes a little unfocused. "I'm fine."

Nacho stepped back. "Uh. What do we do?"

Right away, my mom's first-aid training popped into my head. "Where does it hurt?" I asked the woman.

"My elbow."

With Nacho's help, I got her sitting on the bottom step. The old white lady cradled her hurt arm.

"Ice," I said. "We need ice."

Glancing back the way we'd come, Nacho said, "The corner store. They'll have some."

While he was off on his errand, I called 9-1-1 and reported her fall. No sooner had I disconnected than my phone chimed with a text from Frankie:

Frankie: Where r u? Pierce getting annoyed.

Me: Helping little old lady.

Frankie: Ha ha. That's boy scouts, not rangers.

Me: Serious.

I briefly explained the situation and told her we were waiting for the paramedics to show up. By that time, Nacho had returned with a plastic bag full of ice, so we did our best to make the injured woman comfortable.

She alternated our improvised ice pack between elbow and forehead.

Racking my brain for my mom's first-aid procedures, I asked, "Um, are you feeling dizzy? Do you know what day it is?"

Old Lady shot me a look sharp enough to slice cheese. "I'm banged up, not senile." She gave our uniforms a quick up-and-down. "Earning your Senior Care merit badge or something?"

"No," said Nacho. "That's Boy Scouts. Rangers don't care about old people."

Old Lady scowled. "They've got lots of company. You should hear what those jerks at Medicare make me do."

It took less than ten minutes for the EMTs to arrive, by which time we'd learned more about old people's problems than we'd ever believed possible. As they were loading her into the back of the emergency vehicle, Old Lady was still ranting about her inability to sleep and her uncontrollable farting.

"Feel better soon," I called after her.

"That'll be the day," she said as the ambulance doors closed.

Nacho winced. "Remind me never to get old."

A black SUV pulled to the curb. When the window

buzzed down, it revealed Mr. Pierce's face frowning out at us.

"Get in."

Neither of us wanted to sit beside him, so we both piled into the back seat. My breath caught in my chest. Why the special attention?

Laying an arm across his seat back, Mr. Pierce half turned to face us. His laser gaze bored right through me. I was sure he could tell we'd been visiting the arcade.

"So, doing your good deed for the day?" His voice was mild.

"Yeah," said Nacho, fidgeting. "You know. A Ranger's duty."

"You didn't have to come get us," I said. "We were just about to head back."

Pierce's face gave nothing away. "Uh-huh."

Putting the car into gear, he pulled away from the curb. I perched on the edge of my seat. Was he taking us to Ranger Jail? After a couple of turns, though, it became apparent that we were headed for the middle school. I sat back and relaxed.

"How long did it take the paramedics to show up?" asked Mr. Pierce.

"Not long," I said. "Ten minutes or so."

His eyes flicked up to watch us in the rearview mirror. "The meeting ended ten minutes ago."

"Um, yeah . . ." said Nacho.

Smoothly piloting his car onto the street that ran past the school, Pierce said, "All the other teams returned with plenty of time to spare."

"Oh?" My voice came out squeaky.

"Even after factoring in your good deed, a more suspicious man might wonder what took you so long."

Gulp.

I didn't dare look at Nacho. "We, uh, had some trouble with the compass."

"Yeah," Nacho seconded. "Pathfinding is hard."

Pierce said nothing, letting the silence stretch. He pulled to the curb.

I grabbed the door handle, but before I could open it, our troopmaster spoke again.

"You'll have to repeat the exercise to get your achievement badge."

"Of course," I said.

His shrewd eyes met mine in the mirror. "And next time?"

"Yes?"

"No detours."

Nacho and I fought to keep our faces blank.

"I will know if you deviate from the course," said Mr. Pierce, "and your punishment will be swift and sudden. Are we clear?"

"Yes, sir!" said Nacho and I.

We scooted out of that back seat so fast, I'd swear we left cartoony balls of dust behind us. Watching as Mr. Pierce drove off, I drew a shaky breath.

"That was close. Lucky he had no proof."

But Nacho looked thoughtful. "I still say we need to take him down a peg."

Despite that little voice inside warning me not to poke the tiger, I was still annoyed that my mom wanted to go out with this guy. "Oh, don't worry," I said. "We will."

11

Advice from a Firebug

One downside of having divorced parents is that sometimes you feel a bit like a football, passed back and forth according to their needs. That weekend was supposed to be my makeup time with Dad, since he was traveling and missed a weekend last month. But instead, he, Shasta, and her twins had plans to visit San Francisco. Did they invite me? No way.

They just passed the ball to Mom (*catch, Mari!*) and I spent the weekend at her house instead. Way to make a guy feel wanted, Dad.

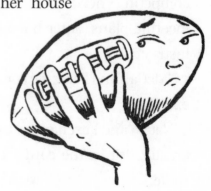

And the worst part? He didn't even *like* visiting cities. He'd much rather go to Big Sur or Joshua Tree.

It only strengthened my resolve to get my parents back together. Just as soon as I could come up with a new, improved plan.

When we gathered for that Saturday's meeting, it was crystal clear who the hard-core Rangers were. During the past week, on their own time, Brayden, Bridget, and José had completed the requirements for some extra achievement badges.

Brayden (no surprise) had finished Wood Carving, finally putting that knife of his to good use. José had ticked off the prerequisites for Cooking, while Bridget claimed to have qualified for Chess, Fingerprinting, and Welding.

(I was sure welding would be super-helpful on our campout.)

They crowded around Mr. Pierce as soon as he arrived, asking him to certify them. With so many competing needs, our troopmaster changed our meeting plans. After having us fall in, he barked out instructions.

"McCall and Perez, go complete your last pathfinding exercise."

Nacho and I exchanged a quick glance. Was another arcade visit in the cards? I could barely restrain my smile.

Pierce passed us a sheet of instructions. "Here's your new destination. And before you go, let's do a little Find My Phone exchange, so I can keep track of you."

My smile wilted.

"Martinez, Ramsey, and Miss Click, bring your documents up to the front so I can certify you."

"What about the rest of us, sir?" asked Nate.

Mr. Pierce scratched his jaw, no doubt weighing different forms of torment. "You? Practice your marching and drills. Miss Patel, you're in charge."

I could tell Frankie really wanted to roll her eyes, but with him staring right at her, she managed to restrain herself.

"Chop-chop!" said Mr. Pierce. "Troop . . . fall out!"

Everyone went about their business as ordered. After giving our fearless leader the means to keep an eye on us, Nacho and I trudged off on our pathfinding exercise. This time around, it was a much shorter course, so we were out and back in no time.

"Ah, the wanderers return," said Mr. Pierce as I handed him the ceramic frog he'd hidden under the orange cone. "Now we can get on with our agenda."

"What badges will we be earning today, sir?" asked Brayden.

"Ah-ah-ah," said the troopmaster, waggling his

swagger stick like a big finger. "Did you think I'd forgotten about your conditioning?"

"Uh, no, sir." Brayden clearly wished he had.

"We'll warm up with seven laps, then switch to push-ups and sit-ups. Double-quick time . . . *march!*"

Maybe it was a mark of how thoroughly he was breaking our spirits, but only two or three Rangers groaned as we set off to work up a sweat.

After fitness conditioning, we broke into small clusters to focus on earning our Fire Safety achievement badge. This badge was particularly important, as Pierce told us the troop couldn't bring any matches on our hike—just the more primitive fire-starting devices. *Very* Bear Grylls.

I was hoping to work with Frankie, since we hadn't hung out today. But somehow I ended up in the group with Xander, Tavia, and Kelvin Chang—the least fire-safe person I knew.

Apparently, Mr. Pierce was a big believer in the teach-yourself method. He dropped off a Ranger Handbook and the necessary materials with each cluster, letting us flounder around on our own while he wandered from group to group, frowning.

Tavia thumbed through the pages, searching for the

fire safety section. When he saw this, Kelvin flapped a hand.

"Pfft," he scoffed. "I know it forward and backward. I can teach you guys."

"Sure you can," said Xander.

"No, really, I know everything there is to know about fires," said Kelvin.

"Except how to put them out," I said.

He sent me an incredulous look through his chunky glasses. "Seriously? You still stuck on that? Ancient history."

"You did light the grass on fire," said Tavia.

"Yeah." Kelvin's eyes sparked behind his glasses. "That was so cool."

"Try dangerous," I said. "Although I'll admit it was kind of exciting, in a we're-all-going-to-die sort of way."

Crossing his thick arms, Xander said, "Okay. Teach us, Firebug."

Laying out the fire-starting kits, Kelvin went through them one by one. "Flint and steel, the old standby." He patted the black rock lovingly, then hefted it and the C-shaped metal piece in his hands. "Strike the flint hard enough at the right angle, and *foof*—instant sparks!"

He wasn't fooling. The wood shavings caught fire right away.

Xander picked up an AA battery from the second kit and peered at it.

"What's that for?" I asked Kelvin. "Does it power some electro-match doohickey?"

Taking the battery from Xander, Kelvin gave it a little kiss, then touched it to a clump of steel wool. Instant flame.

"Whoa," said Xander. "Cool." He blew it out.

"Do you have to kiss it?" Tavia asked.

Kelvin chuckled.

Leaning over the next fire-starting kit, I picked up what looked like a baby bow with a very fat, pointless arrow.

"How's this work?" I asked. "We Robin Hood the fire?"

Kelvin's lip curled. "This," he sneered, "is the world's worst fire starter."

"Of course," I said.

"Why don't we split into two teams?" said Tavia. "Xander and I will use flint and steel, and you guys try that bow thingy."

I rolled my eyes. "Be still, my beating heart."

Showing me how to hold the tools, Kelvin the Pyro said, "See, you put the wood shavings around the base, wrap the bow cord around the dowel, and saw back and forth till you create friction and sparks."

"Does it take long?" I asked.

Kelvin snorted. "Only about two thousand years."

"Bo-o-o-ring!" I said. Then I straightened up, galvanized.

Talking with the world's greatest fire lover had given me an idea. Glancing around, I noticed Mr. Pierce was busy with the knot-tying group, and Tavia and Xander were competing to see how many fires they could start with their flint and steel. I lowered my voice, leaning closer to Kelvin.

"So tell me," I said. "You're into fire, right?"

"Oh, just a little bit." A corner of his mouth curled in a half smile.

"Do you know much about things that go boom?"

The other corner of Kelvin's mouth quirked up. "I might. Like what?"

"A stink bomb?"

His face lit up like Christmas. "Dude," he said, shaking my hand. "You've come to the right dude."

12

Mad Bombers

Like a plague of flesh-eating scarabs, a rain of cock-roaches, a twenty-page math test—or any other kind of cruel torture—Nacho's and my grounding finally came to an end. And not a moment too soon. Summer is no time to be stuck at home. Plus, we had a prank to pull.

Yes, I had finally come up with a way for Nacho and me to teach Mr. Pierce a lesson. And best of all, he'd never know who did it.

The plan came together pretty quickly. First, Kelvin sneaked the necessary chemicals from his summer school chemistry class. Then, my mom and Mr. Pierce made their dinner date for Saturday night when she knew I'd be staying at my dad's. (I know, I should've been working on getting my folks back together, but to be honest, I was fresh out of ideas.)

And finally, Nacho and I tricked Mr. Papadakis into giving us Mr. Pierce's address. (We told him we wanted to write the man a thank-you letter for his leadership. Can you believe he fell for it?)

Kelvin slipped me the materials after our Thursday meeting, so by the weekend, we were all ready to go.

Saturday morning at Dad's house was spent in full-on mad scientist mode, following instructions from Kelvin and a stink bomb recipe he'd found on the Internet. When Shasta McNasty saw us trooping through the kitchen toward the garage, she glanced over from loading the dishwasher.

"What are you boys up to?"

"Oh, just a little chemistry experiment." I hefted the box of supplies. "Hey, you don't happen to have any rubber gloves, do you?"

She smiled, brushing a strand of blond hair from her face. "For a couple of budding scientists? I think I can swing that." Rummaging in a kitchen cabinet, Shasta produced two pairs of gloves. "Will these do?"

"Perfect, Mrs. McCall," said Nacho. He can be smooth with grown-ups when he cares to. "Science thanks you."

"She's not Mrs. McCall," I said. That was my mom's name. "They're not married."

"Yet," said Shasta. "But maybe someday soon."

Not if I had anything to say about it.

Shutting the dishwasher door, she turned on the machine. "I'm just glad you boys are keeping your minds active during summer. What's the project for?"

"Oh, uh . . ." I began. *Oops.* Hadn't thought of a cover story.

"For fun," I said, at the same time Nacho said, "For extra credit."

Confusion crossed Shasta's features. She began to speak, but a wail from the living room claimed her attention. "Don' *wanna* share!" roared either Piper or Zoey. (Who could tell their voices apart?)

"Piper! Play nice with your sister," said Shasta. (Apparently, she could.) "Okay, you boys keep it safe." And she rushed off to deal with her little-kid emergency.

Nacho and I traded a look. "For extra credit?" I said. "In summer?"

"For *fun?*" he said. "Who does chemistry for fun?"

"Kelvin. Did you know he actually *volunteered* for summer school?"

Nacho shook his head. "Different strokes, chamaco." Jerking a thumb toward the garage door, he said, "Shall we?"

I shook off the distracting encounter with Shasta. "To the Batcave!" I cried.

It was a long, messy morning—and a bit too much like school for my tastes—but we finally succeeded in our quest. After all that work, five cool little capsules of stinky goodness sat on my dad's workbench.

"Doesn't look like much," said Nacho.

"But it's got quite a kick," I said, and we both laughed. This was going to be an epic prank.

All through lunch, Nacho and I kept catching each other's eye and cracking up. When Shasta asked what was so funny, I said, "Private joke."

"I wike jokes," said Zoey.

"Okay." I leaned toward her. "Why do gorillas have such big nostrils?"

"Why?" chorused the twins.

I pretended to pick my nose. "Because they have such big fingers."

The girls collapsed in gales of laughter, and Nacho and I joined them, relieved to have an excuse to let it out.

Keeping a straight face during our Rangers meeting proved challenging. Every time I looked at Mr. Pierce, I pictured his reaction to our prank. Somehow that made it easier to endure the jogging, the push-ups, the tire agility exercises, and the rest, knowing that our torturer would soon get his just desserts.

After the workout, our troopmaster called us together at the picnic tables for an announcement. I flopped down on a bench between Frankie and Nacho, wiping sweat from my forehead.

"Probably he's going to announce another hour of torture," said Nacho.

"He's really earning his punishment today," I said.

Frankie leaned forward to look at us both, and a lock of hair fell across her forehead in the most adorable way. "Punishment? What are you guys talking about?"

"Nothing," we chorused. I stifled a smile.

Frankie still looked suspicious, so I continued, "We, uh, figure he'll be spanked by one of those gods with lots of arms for the way he's been treating us. Karma and so forth."

She smirked. "You have no idea what *karma* means, do you?"

"Not a clue," I said.

Mr. Pierce stood before us. "Listen up, Rangers. There's an important position I need to fill."

"Assistant torturer," whispered Nacho, and I almost lost it.

"Every troop needs a senior squad leader," said Mr. Pierce. "Someone who'll serve as a second-in-command, who can help their fellow Rangers succeed."

Thrusting her arm into the air, Bridget said, "I'll do it!"

"She would," Nacho muttered.

"I need to see if any of you rancid pudding monkeys are up to the task," said our troopmaster. "Over the next few weeks, I'll be watching you closely to determine who's worthy."

Up shot Bridget's hand again. "What qualities are you looking for?"

"Leadership, ability, and a good attitude," said Mr. Pierce.

At this, Bridget beamed.

"She thinks it's going to be her," whispered Frankie. Her breath smelled like mint as it tickled my ear. A warm feeling traveled along my spine.

"Uh, yeah," I said. "No doubt." I sure couldn't picture myself or Nacho as senior squad leader.

Clapping his hands, Mr. Pierce said, "All right, let's see if you low-down dookie whistlers are capable of learning anything."

That day, we covered camping skills, like how to set up a tent, cooking over a camp stove, and where to find edible plants. Mostly we followed instructions from the Ranger Handbook while Mr. Pierce scowled at us. (Maybe he thought that was encouragement?) I confess it surprised me to learn we had edible plants growing in the fields below the school grounds. Still, I'd have to be seriously desperate to eat them.

I thought Nacho and I managed to hold it together pretty well through the meeting. It didn't seem like the troopmaster suspected anything. But when Nacho caught my eye during our final lineup and made an I-smell-a-stink face, I lost it.

"McCall!" barked Mr. Pierce. "Rangers don't giggle like little girls when they're at attention."

"Hey!" objected Bridget, Frankie, and Tavia.

"Sorry, ladies," said the ex-Marine. "I'll revise that: Rangers don't giggle." I waited for the push-ups command, but Mr. Pierce gave me a considering look, and at last said, "McCall, take a lap."

For a moment, I paused. If I refused to run and instead complained to my mom about him, would she cancel her date with Pierce?

Doubtful. Mom seemed to enjoy my getting some punishment.

"Well?" said the troopmaster.

I gave him a sarcastic salute. "Aye-aye, sir."

As I jogged, I wondered. It wasn't like him to spare me. Was he feeling a little guilty about going out with my mom? Or maybe he thought he'd do better with her if her son wasn't moaning about torture all the time?

Who knew the workings of a grown-up's mind?

Not me. But I did know one thing for sure: When our troopmaster returned home from his dinner date that night, he was going to get one heck of a surprise.

Dealing with parents is just like cooking: You have to know the right ingredients and the proper order for throwing them together. It took a teaspoon of tricky maneuvering, a dash of begging, and a pinch of truth-bending, but Nacho and I finally managed to arrange our evening. We knew our parents would never agree to let us ride our bikes around after dark, so we used the classic dodge.

Nacho told his moms he was sleeping over at my house, and I told Dad and Shasta I was sleeping over at his.

Turning down their offer of a ride, I packed a few things in a book bag. Right after Nacho and I scarfed down Shasta's vegan lasagna dinner, we took off on our bikes, pedaling slowly through the twilight streets.

"I know she's the devil in a blue sundress, but your dad's girlfriend makes some mean lasagna," said Nacho.

"Yeah, whatever," I said.

And that was part of the problem. Despite her New Agey flakiness, Shasta McNasty *wasn't* the most awful person in the universe. She *did* make good dinners, and she was a decent mom to her little girls. And all of that just interfered with my getting my parents back together.

Grrr.

But I couldn't tell Nacho my plans for reuniting Mom and Dad. Even though we were best friends, he wouldn't get it. He'd just tell me the reunion wasn't going to happen, and I didn't need his negativity right then. Sometimes you have to protect your dreams.

We killed some time in a park near Mr. Pierce's house, waiting for full darkness. Sitting on a bench, I checked my phone. Seven thirty. By now, Mom and the mean green machine would have ordered dinner and been making chitchat, like . . .

Yeah, right.

Anyway, unless he insulted her and she stormed out (a real possibility, given how he treated us kids), Nacho and I had at least another hour for our dirty deed.

I jiggled my feet, feeling antsy as heck.

Like a savvy friend, Nacho read my body language. "Late enough?" he asked.

"It'll have to be."

Collecting our book bags, we pedaled the few blocks to the quiet street where Mr. Pierce's house stood. A long, low dwelling, it stared suspiciously at us from across a broad lawn, watching and waiting.

Or maybe that was just my jitters.

We climbed off our bikes and eyeballed our target. Mr. Pierce had left the front light on, so we'd be clearly visible while doing our prank.

Dang.

Was this a sign? Should we really be doing this? I shook my head, deciding to let Future Coop figure that one out. Present Coop had some pranking to do.

Donning one of the paper masks I'd borrowed from my mom's stash of hospital supplies, I turned to Nacho. "What do you think?"

"Masks aren't enough," said Nacho.

I surveyed the yard. A few waist-high bushes near the curb offered a little cover if we needed it, but from there, the lawn stretched unbroken up to the house. And right now, it was lit up like a stage.

"Shoot," I said. "You're right. What do we do?"

"Turn off the light."

I squinted at the porch wall. "Doesn't look like there's an outside switch."

"Undo the light bulb?" said Nacho.

I shrugged. "That could work."

"You go. You're taller."

Giving him my most sarcastic expression, I said, "Gee, thanks a bunch."

"De nada, dude," said Nacho.

We checked the street. No cars coming, and the last light was fading from the sky. Butterflies pirouetted in my stomach. It was now or never.

"Here I go," I said.

"Good luck."

Approaching the front door, I checked out the porch lamp. It was one of those basic ones with a glass dome that covered the bulb and screwed into the base. No outdoor switch to be seen. I'd have to unscrew the stupid thing.

Standing on tiptoes, I stretched and grabbed the dome.

"Hot, hot!" I cried, snatching my hand back.

"Shhh!" Nacho hissed.

Popping my singed fingers into my mouth, I considered the problem. Where could I find something to protect my hand?

"Your T-shirt," said Nacho, crouching by the bushes.

I whipped the shirt off and wrapped it around my hand. With the added protection, I was able to unscrew the dome and set it down. Now, to—

"Car!" cried Nacho.

I froze.

Headlights sliced the darkness, moving our way. Was it Mr. Pierce, back too soon?

13

All Stunk Up

A blast of adrenaline shot through my limbs. I started to join Nacho behind the bushes, then realized that the driver couldn't miss seeing me if I sprinted across that lawn.

What to do?

Spinning back toward the door, I crouched down and pretended to be examining the potted ficus tree that stood beside it. The back of my neck burned. I could feel the driver's hot gaze on me.

But I kept my face turned toward the house, and within

seconds I heard the car pass by, continuing up the street. It wasn't Mr. Pierce.

Nerves jangling like wind chimes in a hurricane, I let out my breath and stood up.

"Hurry!" cried Nacho.

"Shhh!"

I glanced both ways. All clear for now. Going up on tiptoes again, I grabbed the light bulb in my T-shirt-wrapped hand.

"Yow, still hot," I muttered. But the bulb loosened and the light went out. Screwing the dome back in place, I slipped on my T-shirt and hustled over to rejoin Nacho.

You had to hand it to him. After I'd told him our plan, he'd come up with a way to make the prank even more awesome.

Reaching into his backpack, Nacho snagged the jumbo bag of uncooked spaghetti noodles he'd brought from home. "I'll get started with these babies while you place the stink bombs," he said. Nacho's grin gleamed in the dimness. "He's gonna freak!"

"Like the Joker when Batman wins," I agreed.

"You know," said Nacho. "This is the most organized we've ever been."

I nodded. "I guess Pierce is having a positive effect on us after all."

We both cackled.

Ever so carefully, I removed the zippered baggie with the stink bomb capsules from my knapsack's zippered pouch. Bombing myself was not part of the plan.

After another swift glance along the road, I hustled up to Mr. Pierce's front door. A broad mat sprawled before it, reading, WELCOME.

Perfect.

Flipping the mat back, I crouched. Moving as carefully as a doctor doing brain surgery, I arranged the five capsules so that our troopmaster would have to step on at least one of them when he came home. Then I gently replaced the mat.

"Psst!" hissed Nacho, kneeling on the lawn.

"What?"

"What if he parks in the garage and enters through an inside door?"

I waved off his comment. "He'll have to come through the front door sometime, right?"

"I guess."

"Anyway," I said, "where else can we hide it?"

At Nacho's shrug, I rose to my feet. But I rose too fast. At the last second, I lost my balance. My arms windmilled as I swayed, but it was no use. One foot automatically stepped back to stabilize me.

Pfft.

Just the faintest of sounds as I stepped onto the welcome mat. And then . . .

"Aaugh!"

I clapped both hands over my mouth and nose, but it was too late. The foulest stink—something like skunk and rotten eggs with a twist of rancid Limburger cheese—instantly surrounded me.

My eyes watered. My nose rebelled and tried to flee my face.

Out onto the lawn I fled, not caring whether the neighbors could see.

"Oh, *man!*" said Nacho. He fanned a hand before his face. "That stinks!"

Coughing, I pulled my T-shirt up to cover my nose. "Mission—*hack*—accomplished."

The stench was so strong, it drove us back across the lawn to the bushes. But Nacho remembered to bring the spaghetti packet along, so we knelt back down on the grass. Strand by strand, we inserted the uncooked pasta into the lawn, where it stood up like a tiny yellow forest.

Although I wished I could rinse out the inside of my nose (or maybe chop it off), the smell wasn't quite so mind-blowing from farther away. We were able to keep planting spaghetti.

"So," I said, "the stink capsules work."

"You think?" said Nacho.

"We'll have to thank Kelvin."

Steadily plugging noodles into the lawn, Nacho said, "Huh. He's really on a date with your mom?"

"Kelvin?" I said, though I knew what he was talking about.

"Mr. Pierce, dummy," said Nacho.

The sheepshank knot that had been tied in my stomach all week gave another twist. "Yeah."

"Man, that's messed up."

I bit my lip. Sometimes that's all you need to hear— that someone you know and trust feels the same way you do. That you're not crazy or unreasonable.

I nodded, grateful.

We kept working in silence. When another car's headlights shone down the road, we were too far from the bushes to hide. So we face-planted onto the lawn.

"Don't see us, don't see us, don't see us," chanted Nacho under his breath.

I raised my head slightly to watch the car pass by. "Jedi mind trick?"

"These are not the troublemakers you're looking for," said Nacho, in a pretty decent Obi-Wan Kenobi impression. It reminded me how my dad and I used to watch the original *Star Wars* movies together, nearly every month.

Whether the Force helped us or not, we avoided detection. When the car pulled out of sight, Nacho and I got up and resumed planting pasta. We were able to cover about two-thirds of the lawn before running out of spaghetti.

"Good enough?" asked Nacho.

"I think we made our point," I said, glancing at my phone.

Now my stomach was in knots for a different reason: We were pushing the edge of our window of safety. Almost an hour had passed. Who knew it took so long to plant spaghetti and stink bombs?

"Let's bounce," said Nacho.

We were just lucky that Mr. Pierce hadn't returned already. But it was kind of a good news/bad news situation.

Stowing the paper masks back in my knapsack, we hurried to our bikes and pedaled off into the night. After a couple of blocks, my shoulders finally relaxed.

"Whew!" I said. "That was intense."

"That was *wicked*!" hooted Nacho. "Legendary!"

I laughed. "I wish we'd planted a nanny cam, so we could see his reaction."

If only I'd known: Be careful what you ask for.

I was so pumped from our adventure that my nerves were still buzzing like flies on fresh roadkill by the time we reached my dad's house. Fun had been in short supply since we'd gotten grounded, and this adventure definitely filled the void.

"See ya mañana, chamaco!" I called, waving to Nacho.

"Later, chamaco!" he said, pedaling onward.

Leaving my bike in front of the house, I strolled in through the front door, feeling pretty good about myself.

"Coopah!" cried the twins, running to greet me. They might have been demon spawn, but they were pretty darned cute, I had to admit.

"Hey, munchkins," I said, hugging them and ruffling their hair.

"Pee-yew!" said Piper.

"You stink!" Zoey pinched her nose.

"Coop?" said my dad, materializing in the doorway behind them. "I thought you were spending the night at Nacho's."

Whoops.

I'd totally forgotten to come up with a cover story.

"Uh . . ." Thinking fast, I finally managed, "We, uh, hung out for a while, but they, uh, had a problem with their cesspool."

As the last of the stink reached my dad, he wrinkled his nose. "So I smell."

"Plus, I felt bad about skipping a night with you guys. So I came on back."

Dad's face revealed a trace of suspicion behind his smile. But Shasta popped up behind him with "Oh, that's so sweet. Why didn't you call us for a ride? We would've come to get you."

"I, uh, didn't want to bug you."

Stepping forward, she squeezed my arm. "Well, your timing is perfect. How'd you like to read the girls a bedtime story?" Shasta sniffed delicately. "After you change your clothes?"

I scratched my jaw, thinking it over. Our deed was done. Nothing remained but to wait and hear how awesomely our prank turned out. I felt charitable toward the world, even including my dad's second family.

"You know what?" I smiled down at the twins. "There's nothing I'd like more."

14

Pierce's Punishment

I thought it would be a sweet agony, like waiting to open gifts on Christmas morning. I thought I'd need to spend hours practicing my deadpan face, so I wouldn't give anything away when I heard the news. But it turned out, Nacho and I didn't have long to wait.

Midafternoon on Sunday, I was sprawled on the couch, doodling in my sketch pad as *Adventure Time* played in the background. I was sketching some of my fellow Rangers, but I was no closer to coming up with a brilliant idea for my first graphic novel.

Then my dad walked in. From his tight shoulders and frown, I could tell something was up.

"Everything okay?" I asked.

His frown deepened. "Tell me this isn't you." I noticed he held his cell phone in a death grip.

It could only be about last night's prank, but I

was pretty sure that the passing cars hadn't witnessed anything incriminating. I decided to play Mr. Innocent. "What are you talking about?" I asked, sitting up.

My dad raised his phone, tapped it once, and showed me the screen. A black-and-white video clip played. In it, someone in a surgical mask walked up close to the camera, reached for something just above the frame, and said, "Hot, hot!"

That someone was me.

Double-dog-dang it. Pierce had a spy camera covering his front stoop. This was the *second* time I'd been undone by an unseen security camera.

"Uh . . ." My mind raced. He'd probably hidden it somewhere up in the branches of the potted ficus.

"Why?" My dad's voice pierced like a lance. "Why, after all that's happened, your grounding and everything? *Why* would you do this?"

The video played on. Despite my having unscrewed Pierce's porch light, you could still make out Nacho and me fleeing the stink and planting spaghetti.

I tried a laugh, and it came out phony. "It was just a joke, a prank."

"A prank?" My dad's pale face reddened.

"Yeah, like how football players TP their coach's house," I said, feeling sweat beading up at my hairline. "All in good fun."

Dad's fist landed on his hip. "Oh, so it's *fun* to make someone clean up spaghetti from their lawn?"

Finally, I couldn't help myself. "He deserved it!"

"What?"

"He's mean, and he's dating Mom!" I cried. "I couldn't just do nothing."

For a moment, silence. Dad's lips pursed and he drew a long breath through his nose. "Run that by me again?"

"He's dating Mom. They went out to dinner last night, and we've got to stop him before it gets serious."

"No." Dad's head was shaking before I even finished. "No, we don't."

"But—"

"We're divorced. Your mother can date whoever she likes."

I couldn't believe I was hearing this. "But Mr. *Pierce?*"

Rubbing his neck, my dad said, "Even Mr. Pierce. She has a right to be happy."

"But she's happiest with you."

Something flashed across my dad's face—regret, maybe?—and he said, "Not anymore." Then his frown reappeared. "So you decided to prank your troopmaster to break them up?"

I shrugged. "I . . ."

"Honestly, Cooper. Do you ever think before you act?"

Not usually.

I hung my head. "I'm sorry."

And I *was* sorry—sorry we'd been caught. Sorry my dad wasn't bothered by my mom dating someone else. Sorry that I couldn't seem to figure out how to get them back together.

"That doesn't cut it, bub," Dad said.

I couldn't meet his eyes. "Am I . . . grounded again?" Dread coiled in my stomach like a dragon in a cave.

"No," he said.

"Really?" Sudden relief flooded me.

Dad's arms crossed. "We're not punishing you this time."

A chuckle burst from my throat. "Dad, I'm so—"

"We're leaving that to Mr. Pierce," he said.

For a moment, I couldn't speak. "P-Pierce?"

"He's the injured party, so he gets to decide." Dad's smile was entirely without sympathy. "Good luck, buddy boy. You're going to need it."

Monday morning, bright and early, Mom drove Nacho and me to Mr. Pierce's house. It looked different in the daytime (and without pasta all over the lawn).

Smaller. Sadder somehow.

Sitting in the car, Nacho and I traded glances. Neither one of us wanted to move.

"Come on," said my mom. "No use postponing it."

Dragging my legs like they were locked in old-fashioned irons, I shuffled out of the car and up the driveway. Nacho's feet scuffed the pavement beside mine. We exchanged another hangdog look.

We were really in for it this time.

Mom, on the other hand, practically bounded up to the front door. When Mr. Pierce swung it open, I almost didn't recognize that thing on his face.

A smile.

He was grinning at my mom like she was a banana split with fudge and nuts and a cherry on top. And as I stopped beside her, I saw Mom's answering smile.

Yuck.

"Hey, Mari," he said.

"Rocky," she replied.

Nacho caught my eye. *Rocky?* he mouthed. But I was more concerned with the flirty tone in my mom's voice and the way they were looking at each other. That didn't bode well *at all.*

"Here are your troublemakers," Mom said. "Do with them what you will."

"Hey!" I said.

She turned to me, and the smile had vanished like the last slice of peach pie. "You earned every bit of it, mister. I told Rocky—Mr. Pierce—that he has free rein to punish you. As long as he doesn't draw blood, anything is fair game."

Nacho's eyes bugged out. I'm pretty sure mine did too, even though I was certain she was joking. Well, almost certain.

"Mom!" I protested.

"Okay, I'm off to work." She kissed Mr. Pierce's cheek. I winced.

"If I'm done with them before two o'clock, I'll drop these two pranksters at your house," said Mr. Pierce. "Assuming there's anything left."

"Oh, ha-ha," I said. But he'd never joked before, so why was I laughing?

With a little finger wave, Mom turned and sauntered off, and we were left to the tender mercies of the mean green machine.

"Rangers, atten . . . *hut!*" barked our troopmaster.

What could we do? Nacho and I snapped to attention.

"Now . . ." said Mr. Pierce. Back straight, chest up, he bounced on his heels and stared down at us with narrowed eyes.

The suspense was killing me. Was he going to whack us with his riding crop?

"I thought long and hard about what punishment would fit the crime," said Mr. Pierce. "Bamboo shoots under the fingernails? Thumbscrews? Keelhauling?"

My insides turned to sand. Wasn't it illegal to torture tweens? How could my mom leave me with this guy?

"But then I thought of something even better," said our troopmaster.

"Sir?" asked Nacho, unable to contain himself.

The man's slit-eyed smile was borderline sinister. "Hard labor."

Gulp.

"Excuse me," I said, "sir?"

Pierce's smile broadened. "You may have noticed this house is a little run-down. I only moved in last month, and haven't had time to do much."

My head swiveled to check out the front yard. It seemed pretty tidy to me, especially without the spaghetti. The grass was neatly trimmed and edged. The bushes weren't too shaggy.

"Not the front yard. Follow me, you pathetic fudge nuggets," said Mr. Pierce, executing a smooth about-face.

With a worried glance at me, Nacho followed. I fell in behind.

Inside, the house was scary neat and uncluttered. We passed a living room with a couch, two armchairs, and a sweet wide-screen TV, all in shades of black or gray. A hall led away from it to the left, and through a half-open door on our right lay what looked like a home office, complete with walnut desk and fancy computer. Almost nothing hung on the walls, just a few certificates and a framed poster of some tough-looking boxer.

Under the image, it read:

> **It's repetition of affirmations that leads to belief. Once that belief becomes a deep conviction, things begin to happen.**
> **—Muhammad Ali**

But Pierce skipped the guided tour. Instead, he led us through a small, tidy kitchen and into the backyard.

Or should I say, the toxic waste dump?

My jaw dropped. The place was a disaster area. Rusty, busted patio furniture and what looked like a defunct washing machine sprawled in agony among waist-high weeds, like fallen soldiers. Looking closer, I spotted an old truck tire, a deflated inflatable pool, and other random trash peeking out. A solitary dead tree presided over the whole mess.

"Rangers . . . halt!" barked Mr. Pierce.

We stopped. I can't speak for Nacho, but my heart sank all the way to my socks. This was no minor punishment. This was a month's worth of mess to clean up. Surely he didn't expect us to handle it all.

"What, uh, what exactly do you want us to do?" I asked. When Pierce lifted an eyebrow, I added, "Sir."

"As you can see, this yard is a fixer-upper," said our troopmaster. "I only had time to fix up the front."

"I guess," said Nacho, forgetting the "sir."

"You two dipsticks are going to make this area ship-shape again."

"But that'll take forever!" I protested.

Mr. Pierce's eyes narrowed. "Maybe you should have thought of that before you planted pasta in my lawn."

Yeah, like the state of his backyard had ever figured into our prank planning. I rolled my eyes.

"Oh, and I found your stink bombs," said our troop-master. "A little tip?"

"Sir?" said Nacho.

"If you set one of them off before the prank, it spoils the surprise."

Oh, great. He didn't even step on the other ones? So much for teaching him a lesson.

Mr. Pierce indicated a wheelbarrow, gardening tools, and two sets of gloves. "There's your equipment."

I gulped. "Where do we start?"

"First, haul all the bigger trash out to the curb for pickup," he said. "Then pull the weeds—and make sure you remove all those roots. I don't want them growing back. After you're done with all that, we'll talk about the tree."

"Oh-kayyy . . ." said Nacho, clearly stunned by the amount of work ahead of us.

Mr. Pierce started back inside, then pivoted on his heel at the doorway. "I'll be in my office. And remember: no lollygagging. I've got eyes in the back of my head."

I didn't doubt it for a second. He probably had a backyard spy camera too.

Nacho looked like his favorite dog had just run off to join the Iditarod. "This summer just keeps getting better and better."

I rubbed my forehead. "I know. I'm actually beginning to think we might be better off toeing the line for a while."

Nacho didn't even object. He just gave the mother of all heavy sighs.

And with that, we put on the gloves and got down to work.

15

Don't Get Bitten by a Bear

After that first day of hard labor, my back ached, my neck was sunburned, and my knees throbbed from kneeling. Four and a half hours of sweat (with twenty minutes off to wolf down a peanut butter and jelly sandwich for lunch), and we barely put a dent in the job. I mean, yeah, we hauled all the heavy stuff to the curb and bundled the other trash into bags, but we'd hardly started the weeding.

This was going to take awhile.

During our first day's punishment, we learned a few tidbits about the mysterious Mr. Pierce. For one thing, he couldn't cook (as witnessed by the PB&Js). For another, our troopmaster had worked in cybersecurity while in the Corps, and was now consulting for several companies in town.

I wished we'd known that *before* we decided to prank his fortress.

But the main thing I learned about Mr. Pierce, I didn't piece together until I was lying in bed that night nursing my sore muscles. I thought about his house. The man had no art on the walls and hardly any furniture; no kids; few friends; and he'd agreed to lead a woeful troop of Rangers before even meeting us. When I added it all up, I came to one conclusion:

Mr. Pierce was a serial killer.

(Either that, or lonely.)

Rolling onto my side, I gazed out at the half-moon. What to make of this information? On the one hand, it made me feel a little sorry for the man. On the other hand, I really wished he'd stop using my mom to feel less alone. Oh, and also stop torturing Nacho, me, and the other Rangers.

It was a lot to process.

Tuesday ended up worse than Monday, which I didn't think was possible. Not only did we spend another four hours pulling the gnarliest, thorniest, stubbornest weeds I'd ever met, but also, we had to ride with Mr. Pierce to the Rangers meeting.

Being alone with him in close quarters was a little bit scary—like riding shotgun with a grizzly bear. Plus, nothing says "I'm a total suck-up" like being chauffeured to a Rangers meeting by your troopmaster.

When we arrived, Nacho and I lagged behind Mr. Pierce on the walk from the car, hoping nobody would notice we'd come with him.

Fat chance.

"Hey, Coop," Frankie greeted me. "Bucking for the senior squad leader job, are we?"

I waved off her comment. "Nah, he just, uh, gave us a ride. My mom was, um, busy."

Her eyebrows rose. "So now Mr. Pierce is offering taxi service for Rangers? Sweet. Maybe he'll take me shopping."

I tried a laugh. It came out phonier than an excuse note I once wrote in crayon, back in second grade.

"It's just, uh . . ." I had run out of excuses.

Frankie grinned. "Don't worry, I already know the whole story."

"You do?"

"I can't believe you actually set off your own stink bomb," she said, giggling. "Who does that?"

Behind her, Kelvin was shaking his head with a pitying look. "Dude. After all I've done for you."

I could only shrug.

Luckily, Mr. Pierce spared me from further

embarrassment by ordering us to fall in. For the first time ever, I was grateful that we had to stand still, staring straight ahead. It kept me from seeing my fellow Rangers' pitying faces.

"Troop, there's only ten days left before our camping trip," said Mr. Pierce. "That's just five meetings to get you miserable kumquat chuckers ready to face the wilderness." He shook his head. "I doubt you can pull it off."

"We'll be ready, sir!" said Bridget Click.

The ex-Marine lifted an eyebrow. "Oh, really? Martinez, what's the first rule of backpacking?"

"Um, don't get bitten by a bear, sir?" said José.

"Wrong. Miss Patel?"

Frankie straightened up. "Leave no trace?" she said.

"Excellent." The troopmaster emphasized his words by thwacking his riding crop into his palm. "Leave. No. Trace. That means you pack out what you pack in. No trash left behind. And you leave the campsite looking better than you found it. Understood?"

"Yes, sir," we replied.

"Now, if you're going to hike up a mountainside in ten days without dying, you better get in shape. Time for some cardio."

"Question, sir?" said Nate.

"Yes, Burns," said Mr. Pierce.

"What are the other rules of backpacking?" he asked. I suspected Nate was trying to delay the inevitable.

"Excellent question," said the troopmaster. "And you'll learn the answer after your physical conditioning. But first, let's pump you up."

Excuse me?

"Who's the best troop?" barked Mr. Pierce.

"Troop Nineteen!" we yelled.

"I can't *hear* you."

"Troop Nineteen!"

And on it went until he judged us sufficiently pumped. Then our troopmaster tucked his riding crop under his arm and shouted, "Troop, about . . . *face!*"

We spun on our heels, more or less together, until we were facing the opposite direction.

"Forward, march!" barked Mr. Pierce. Even before we found our rhythm, he barked, "Double-quick time . . . *march!*" And away we trotted.

When I got back home that day, I felt like I'd gone jogging in the Gobi Desert. All I wanted was to drink an ocean or two of Gatorade and take a long nap.

Nevertheless, the sound of a wailing guitar greeted me as I walked through the door. So much for napping.

Nana C was working up a new tune for her band, something that was already an oldie when my dad was born.

"Hey, Nana C!" I called.

"Coop?" she said from the front room. "Come give your old gran a hug."

When I walked in, she was setting her cherry-red electric guitar into its stand. I noticed she'd added a blue stripe to her hair. *Go, Nana.* We hugged, and she asked how things were going.

"Okay, I guess."

Nana C brushed back the hair from my forehead and met my eyes. "No," she said, "they're not. What's *really* going on?"

I tried turning away, but her hand on my shoulder held me steady. Playing guitar gave her a grip like iron.

"It's Mom," I said. "She's dating."

Her blue eyes widened and her mouth curved into a smile. "Well, good for her."

"Yeah, but she's dating my troopmaster." I looked away. "It's . . . weird."

Nana C kept her laser gaze on me. I swear she was using some kind of granny mind meld. "And?"

Fidgeting, I said, "And . . ." The words burst out in a rush. "She can't get back with Dad if she's dating someone else."

"Ah." My grandma's tone was gentle. She sat down on the couch with me. "Coop, you're a smart boy. I bet you've noticed that your dad's got a serious girlfriend."

"Yeah."

"And you know he's helping her raise her girls."

"Yeah."

She patted my hand, saying nothing.

"But don't you want Dad and Mom to be together?" I asked.

Her gaze stayed steady. "I want them to be happy. Whatever form that takes."

"Even if they're not married?" My voice warbled a little, for some reason.

"Even then, kiddo." Nana C gave me a side hug. "I know it's hard. They both love you, but they have their own lives to live too."

I knew that. Of course I knew that. But it didn't help any.

"I still think it totally sucks," I said.

She nodded. "True. But you know what doesn't suck?"

I looked at her sidelong. "What?"

"Fresh snickerdoodle cookies."

Letting my head fall forward, I said, "Fresh chocolate chip cookies suck even less."

She patted my back. "Done and done."

Grandma C was right. Fresh-baked cookies didn't totally suck. I spent a couple of hours doodling in my sketch pad while munching them. Since my brilliant inspira- 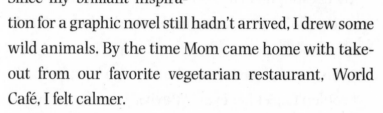 tion for a graphic novel still hadn't arrived, I drew some wild animals. By the time Mom came home with take-out from our favorite vegetarian restaurant, World Café, I felt calmer.

Hustling off to her rehearsal, Nana C gave me a quick squeeze and a kiss. "Take care, kiddo. Things will work out, you'll see."

Over a falafel plate, Mom told me stories about her day, about the confused woman in the recovery room who thought she was Beyoncé, and about the guy in the ER who had stuck a candle where the sun don't shine and couldn't get it out again. Never a shortage of weirdness at the hospital.

"And how was your day?" she asked, taking a bite of Greek salad.

"It . . . um . . ." I tried to tell her, but couldn't erase the mental image of her smooching Mr. Pierce's cheek.

Mom reached out and touched my hand. "What is it?"

I thought about what my grandma had said. But then I thought, *Grown-ups don't know everything.*

"It's Mr. Pierce," I said. "He's totally mean."

"You did spaghetti-fy his lawn," she said. "I think he has a right to be angry. Don't you?"

My chest tightened. Now that my chance had come, why couldn't I just say what I was thinking? "Yeah, no. It's . . ."

"This is about me having dinner with him, isn't it?"

I couldn't meet her eyes. "Maybe."

"Honey boy, look at me." When I met her gaze, she said, "It was just a dinner. I've had dinner dates with some other guys since your dad and I split up."

I rocked back in my chair. "Really?" This was news to me.

She sighed. "I know it's weird for you. It's weird for me too."

"But . . ."

"I didn't introduce them to you because, well, things never got serious enough," she said. "And because I didn't want *this* to happen."

"Oh." It was a lot to process.

"I thought you were mature enough to handle me dating now. Coop, you can't just go planting spaghetti in the yard of every guy I go out with."

Why not?

Fiddling with my falafel, I said, "It's not just that."

It was almost totally that.

Mom set her fork down. "Then what is it?"

"Mr. Pierce is cruel. He calls us names, and he makes us do stuff we don't want to. It's totally unfair."

"That's what discipline looks like," she said. "Although I plan to have a word with him about the name-calling."

"Can I please quit the Rangers?"

Taking another bite of salad, Mom said, "Yes."

"Really?" I went limp. Relief flooded my veins. I wanted to give her a big, sloppy—

"If you're ready to give up on your cartooning camp."

And relief instantly flooded out. "Mom . . ."

"Eat your hummus, honey boy." She pushed my plate closer. "You're not done with the Rangers by a long shot."

16

Perkiness Attack

The next nine days flew by like a tornado on a ten-speed Schwinn. We worked on achievement badges and read the Ranger Handbook, which was so dull it should be used to cure insomnia. We jogged, hiked the hills, and tried to get in shape. Almost nobody had camping equipment, so Mr. Pierce promised to get a friend of his to donate some military surplus gear. Between that and Mr. Papadakis's offer of sleeping bags at wholesale prices, we were outfitted at last.

Bridget was so excited about the camping trip, she checked about ten different weather apps, searching for the perfect weekend. In the end, she told Mr. Pierce that his original pick was the weekend most likely to be rain-free.

Brayden carved what he called the "ultimate walking stick," and Kelvin had visions of creating the most enormous bonfire ever. It was safe to say the troop was getting pumped up.

Through it all, Nacho and I continued cleaning up our troopmaster's backyard. It was backbreaking work—especially chopping down the dead tree— but we finally finished up the day before the camping trip.

That afternoon, Nacho and I went with our moms to buy supplies for our adventure. Mr. Pierce had given us a list including everything from freeze-dried food to flint and steel to first-aid kits. Because Mrs. Perez said that real food was better for us than what she called "that horrible camping food," we ended up shopping at Costco.

Nacho took one look at the list and curled his lip. "You call this food? Where are the Oreos? The nacho chips? It's missing all the basic food groups."

"I know."

"And this freeze-dried stuff? Hah!" he scoffed.

"Yeah, I get enough chicken à la king at school," I said. "And dried apricots are just nasty."

"Anyway, these are only suggestions," said Nacho. "Forget this list. Let's get what we want."

What we wanted ended up being heavy on our favorite foods and light on just about everything else.

Forty-five minutes later, we staggered out of there with enough packages, boxes, and cans to feed the entire population of Dubuque. When we got home, a pile of camping gear waited on our front stoop, courtesy of Mr. Pierce's friend.

Nacho put his hands on his hips. "Hijole, dude. Which army used this stuff, the Salvation Army?"

"Seriously," I said.

"How much you think we could get for it at a pawnshop?" said Nacho, turning up his nose at the camouflage-patterned packs and tent.

"Bus fare, maybe," I said.

On the outside, I was trying to be scornful like Nacho, but inside, the part of me that enjoyed nature walks with my dad was thrilled by the new equipment. We had never actually camped overnight, so the tent and backpack seemed pretty cool.

Dragging the gear into my living room, Nacho and I divvied up our food and crammed it into the backpacks. By the time we'd strapped on our sleeping rolls and added all the clothing, cans, pots, pans, boxes, and bags, the packs were so heavy we could barely stagger.

"Ugh," I grunted. "I feel like that Greek guy who had to carry the world on his back."

Nacho tightened his bellyband. "Tell you one thing: It better be a short hike, or we're all gonna die from heart attacks."

"Then we'll be the Troop of the Living Dead."

Nacho grinned. "Ooh, Zombie Rangers."

"It'd almost be worth dying to see that," I said.

But honestly, though I couldn't tell Nacho this, part of me was eager for a real wilderness adventure. I wondered, what would it be like to actually sleep under the stars?

*   *   *

The next day, Friday, everyone met at the middle school right after lunch, our parents' cars jammed full of gear. Mr. Pierce made us fall in while the grown-ups watched from the sidelines.

"Troop, parade . . . *rest!*" our troopmaster barked.

We responded by putting our hands behind our backs and spreading our feet wider. I wouldn't say we were in unison yet, but hey, we were a lot more coordinated than at the first couple of meetings. When I glanced over at Mom, she raised her eyebrows and nodded, looking impressed.

She had no idea.

"Rangers, welcome to the start of your first outdoor adventure," said Mr. Pierce, sounding a lot friendlier now that other adults were present. No *microbes* or *cheesemongers* now. "We have a two-and-a-half-hour journey ahead of us. I'll take most of you in my SUV, but Mrs. Click has volunteered to drive the rest."

A cheerful-looking, round-bodied woman on the sidelines gave us a finger wave. "I wanted to visit my cousin in Big Bear anyway, so it's no problem to drop you off."

"Think she'd take *me* to Big Bear instead?" whispered Nacho.

I smirked.

"We're only making one stop, so if you need to hit the head, now's your chance," Mr. Pierce continued. "Go-time is in fifteen minutes. Troop, fall out!"

While one of the girls and a couple of the guys trotted off to the bathrooms, Mr. Pierce gave us our riding assignments. Nacho ended up with the crew in Mr. Pierce's SUV (poor Nacho!), while I landed in Mrs. Click's car with Frankie, Bridget, and José.

My group lugged its gear to the car and loaded it in. By the time we finished, the cargo area of Mrs. Click's Lexus SUV was so packed, I doubted she could see over it.

"So, we're riding together," said Frankie, shutting the back hatch.

"Seems like," I said.

She glanced both ways, then muttered, "Check this out." Shielding it with one hand, Frankie lifted a pack of matches from her hiking vest pocket. *Contraband.*

"But we're not supposed to—"

With a little smirk, she said, "What Pierce doesn't know won't hurt him."

Ah, a girl after my own heart. I nodded. "Your secret's safe with me. Anything's better than starting a fire with that bow thingy."

"Should be a nice drive." She patted the SUV. "But get ready for a perkiness attack."

"What do you mean?"

As Mrs. Click bustled around the side of the car, Frankie raised her eyebrows, touching a finger to her nose. "Wait and see."

Before I could get Frankie to explain her comment, my mom waved at me from where she was leaning against our car. I strolled over to join her.

"So," she said, "first overnight campout."

I shrugged. "Yeah."

"Fresh air, tall pines . . ."

"Yup, purple mountains' majesty out the wazoo."

Mom brushed my bangs back. "I know it hasn't been easy, honey boy, but you've really applied yourself—spaghetti incident aside. Your dad and I are proud of you."

"Really?"

She dug in her pocket and removed something small. "So we got you this."

When I opened my hand, she dropped into it a compact, heavy pocketknife. Not just any knife either—it was a tomato-red Swiss Army knife, bristling with attachments.

"Wow," I said. "Thanks. I mean, thanks a lot!" I gave her a quick hug.

"Thought it might come in handy where you're going."

"Absolutely." The knife had several blades, a corkscrew, an awl, scissors—everything but a TV remote. "I love it."

Mom beamed and kissed my cheek. "Have fun, Adventure Boy. We'll see you on Sunday."

Just then, a car horn tooted. Frankie called my name, waving me over. Behind the wheel sat Mrs. Click; our ride was ready.

"Bye, Mom." I hustled off to join them.

My first clue of what lay ahead came only two blocks into our trip.

"Okay, kids," chirped Mrs. Click. "We've got soft drinks in the cooler, snacks in the bag"—she patted the soft cooler on the center console between the front seats—"and two and a half hours for tons of fun. Would you like to start with the License Plate Game, the Compliment Game, Car Bingo, or a song?"

"Ooh, a song, a song!" cried Bridget, clapping her hands and literally bouncing in the front seat.

I shot a look at Frankie, sitting between me and José in the back.

"Don't say I didn't warn you," she muttered.

"Bay-beeeeee . . . *shark*, doot doot 'n' doot-doo-doo, baby *shark*, doot doot 'n' doot-doo-doo," sang Mrs. Click and Bridget, complete with hand gestures.

What were we, five years old? I rolled my eyes so hard, they almost got stuck.

It was going to be a looong drive.

But still, I found myself singing along under my breath.

After endless rounds of "99 Bottles of Beer," "Row, Row, Row Your Boat," License Plate Bingo, and enough car games to keep an entire summer camp busy, we finally arrived at our destination. The car pulled off the pavement and onto a short, rutted dirt road between tall firs. Five minutes of bone-rattling bounces later, we stopped in a cleared space where Pierce's SUV had parked.

"This is it?" I asked, glancing around the clearing. On one side, a port-a-potty. On the other, a wooden sign marking the trailhead. "I was expecting something a bit more . . . impressive."

"Just smell that fresh air," Bridget chirped.

Cautiously, I rolled down the window and took a whiff. The sharp tang of pines tinged the breeze, which was a good ten degrees cooler than back home. Climbing out of the car, we stretched our legs and unloaded our massive backpacks. With all the camo, it looked like a going-out-of-business sale at an army surplus store.

"Well, at least the bears won't be able to spot us," said Frankie.

"Can bears even see in color?" I asked.

She shrugged. "What do I look like, NatGeo Junior?"

We waved goodbye to Mrs. Click, and I strolled over to talk with Nacho.

"Good ride, chamaco?" I asked.

"Surprisingly good treats, chamaco. You?"

I glanced back at Mrs. Click's departing car. "Major cuteness overload," I said. "But the snacks were okay."

Stretching out a kink, Nacho put his fists in his lower back and leaned backward. "I am *so* not looking forward to this." He frowned at the treetops. "Aren't those rain clouds?"

"Where?"

"In my backpack." He snorted. "Duh, up in the sky."

Sure enough, some big fluffy cumuli, just like the ones we'd learned about in earth science lessons, mounded at the edge of the faded-blue-jeans sky.

"Didn't Little Miss Type A say this was supposed to be the non-rainy weekend?" Nacho asked.

"I'm sure our fearless leader knows all about it," I said. "He's the hiking expert, right?"

Just then, Pierce gave us a T-minus ten warning, and it was time to get serious about leaving. Frankie and a couple other Rangers did athletic-type stretches. Several kids stood in line to visit the sketchy-looking port-a-potty. Me, I used the bushes.

When at last everyone was ready, Mr. Pierce gave the order to shoulder our packs and fall in. Buckling our bellybands, we staggered into formation. Somehow, my pack had gained a few pounds on the drive up, and I felt every one. Frankie, however, was having no trouble hefting hers. Either she was a much smarter packer than me, or all that soccer playing had given her legs like a superhero.

Mr. Pierce stood before the troop like a monument, sporting his Mountie-style hat and crisp green uniform. The late afternoon sun slanted down through the trees, catching him in a shaft of light. He surveyed us for a long moment.

"This is it, you lazy muffin munchers," he said. "This is where we separate the men from the b—" He caught sight of Bridget and changed tack. "Where we separate the true Rangers from the lollygaggers. This is where we see what you're made of."

"It sure ain't sugar and spice and everything nice," whispered Nacho.

I tried to stifle my smile.

"Are you ready for adventure?" shouted our troop-master.

"Yes, sir!" cried my fellow Rangers.

"Then let's move out. Front line, lead off!"

As the first row peeled away toward the trailhead and my row waited to follow, I took a deep breath. Much as I hated the troop's discipline and Mr. Pierce always pushing us around, I couldn't help but feel a small thrill. It was a beautiful afternoon, and we were headed into the wild.

Into adventure.

"Here goes nothing," mumbled Nacho.

Later, I'd come to realize, my buddy had never been so right.

17

Too Much Adventure

Less than ten minutes into our hike, the complaints began. We climbed a short hill just after leaving the parking lot, and I was panting long before we reached the crest. My pack weighed about as much as a baby apatosaurus, and the straps bit into my shoulders and hips. Sweat streamed down my forehead and into my eyes in a salty river. Both feet felt hot, like someone had slipped burning coals into my shoes.

"My legs hurt," moaned someone ahead of me.

"A mosquito bit me," another Ranger whined.

"How much farther?" said Kelvin.

Bridget Click, however, had a spring in her step. "Let's sing a song," she chirped. "Here we go! Great big globs of greasy, grimy gopher guts, mutilated monkey meat, chopped up baby parakeet . . ." Xander and Nate joined in.

Right behind me, Nacho panted, "Hiking . . . totally . . . sucks."

Despite my aches, I couldn't resist taking the opposite position. "It's usually . . . pretty fun."

"Not when you're . . . carrying . . . a house on your back," Nacho gasped.

Glancing behind, I saw that our once-tight formation had spread out along the trail like Napoleon's army retreating from Russia (the subject of my last history paper). At the very back of the column, José was hunched over, green as an avocado's innards, with hands braced on knees. My guess? He'd just lost his lunch in the shrubbery.

"Troop, halt!" cried Mr. Pierce from somewhere up ahead.

One by one, kids unbuckled their straps, set down their rucksacks, and flopped onto the ground. Some didn't even bother removing their packs first, just keeled over backward on top of them.

Close behind us, Nate Burns turned a beet-red face our way. "How much . . . longer?" he rasped.

Too breathless to answer, I shrugged.

Bridget Click mopped her brow with her neckerchief and glanced back at us. "The map says it's a seven-mile hike to camp."

"And we're halfway?" asked Nate, hope lighting his face.

"I'd say we've gone maybe a half mile," she answered.

Nate collapsed with a moan.

Brayden was even redder than Nate. "I'm *so* hot," he whined, uncapping his water bottle and splashing it over his upturned face.

A little above us, Frankie was leisurely stretching her legs. She seemed as cool as a frozen cucumber, so maybe I should think about playing soccer if I ever wanted to hike again.

Straightening up, Frankie noticed me and gave a mock salute. I raised my water bottle in return.

"I think she likes you." Nacho elbowed me.

"Yeah, right."

He grinned. "Hey, it's cool with me. She's kind of cute, if you go for girl jocks."

"And what's wrong with girl jocks?" That came out sounding defensive, for some reason.

Nacho held up his palms. "Not a thing, lover boy." With a knowing smirk, he turned away to rummage in his pack.

All too soon, Mr. Pierce gave the order for us to "saddle up," as he put it. Hefting my pack onto a boulder, I crouched, slipped my arms through the straps, and staggered to my feet.

Admiring my technique, Nacho did the same.

"Troop, forward . . . march!" Mr. Pierce cried.

"And we've got six and a half more miles?" asked Nacho. "Ay-ay-ay."

"Ay-ay-ay *yi-yi*," I agreed.

The first stream crossing was a real education. No wooden footbridge—not even one of those Indiana Jones rope bridges. Instead, the trail ran down to the water's edge and magically reappeared on the other side. Between lay only rushing water and a few boulders.

The troop stumbled to a halt while Mr. Pierce peered across the river, considering our situation.

"Isn't there a safer place to cross?" I asked no one in particular.

Of course, Bridget replied. "According to the map, this is the only crossing for miles."

"If we turn back now," said Nacho, collapsing onto a boulder while still wearing his pack, "we can make it home for a late dinner."

"Bwak, bwak, bwak!" teased Xander. "Feeling chicken?"

My friend bristled. "I can handle anything you can."

Apparently, our troopmaster decided it was safe to cross. He led the way, hopping from boulder to boulder like a mountain goat, then watching us expectantly from the other side. What else could we do? We followed him.

Nearly half of my fellow Rangers slipped on the rocks at least once, soaking their pant legs to the thighs. Turning to laugh at Kelvin's slip, I stepped into the water myself.

Cold!

Safe on the far bank, Bridget scolded us for our cursing. "Language!"

"That's nothing," said Nacho, balancing precariously on his boulder. "I'm just getting warmed up."

Halfway across the river, Brayden got a crafty look on his face. "Time for a dip!" he cried, jumping into the stream with his pack on. The other Rangers hooted and clapped.

I think he'd planned on just cooling off, but Brayden's feet slipped, his eyes went wide, and he splashed onto his back, floating off downstream.

"Help!" he screamed.

"Undo your bellyband!" cried Frankie.

"Stand up!" I yelled. "It's not deep."

But maybe his pack was too waterlogged or something, because Brayden kept drifting downstream, waving his arms and legs like an overturned beetle. I tried not to laugh at the sight. But then I pictured Brayden going over a waterfall in that position, and my stomach flipped.

"Come on, guys," I cried. "Let's save him!"

All the Rangers on dry land dumped their packs and raced downstream. I splashed through the shallows and joined them, followed closely by Mr. Pierce.

"Heeelp!" yelled Brayden. He ricocheted off a boulder and spun into deeper water.

We ran faster, dodging rocks and trees, trying to outpace the USS *Brayden*. At last, we pulled far enough ahead to cut him off.

"Quick, form a chain!" I shouted.

Xander, Nate, and José waded in from the far bank. From our side, Frankie, Bridget, Nacho, and I splashed into the stream.

Grabbing my belt and wrapping his other arm around a small tree, Pierce ordered, "Hold on to each other! One kayaker in this crew is enough."

Everyone joined hands. Bridget was closest to the middle of the stream.

Bracing one foot on a boulder and stretching out an arm, she cried, "Take my hand!"

But Brayden was still doing his flailing beetle thing and totally missed her grab. Luckily, Bridget snagged his backpack. With a grunt, she hauled Brayden onto the boulder like a great green-and-khaki fish.

We raised a ragged cheer.

Then slowly, one by one, we passed him along the chain to the shore. As Brayden reached me, he muttered, "I only wanted to cool off."

"Next time, lose the backpack first," I said.

As Mr. Pierce helped Brayden onto dry land and removed his pack, the rest of us joined him. Brayden looked like a drowned rat, but aside from being drenched through and through, he didn't seem to be hurt.

"Ten-minute break to change socks," said Mr. Pierce, glancing up at the sun. "There's still a lot of ground to cover."

Grumbles greeted this remark, but everyone did as he suggested.

Peeling off my wet socks, I fished a dry pair from my pack. "Don't know what good it'll do. My boots are soaked through."

"Poor baby," said Frankie. "Join the club."

"Good thing you put all your gear in a trash bag," Bridget told the miserable Brayden. "You did double-bag your gear, right?"

His sickly smile was all the answer needed.

"Were we supposed to?" Kelvin asked. "No one told me."

"Me neither," said Nacho.

I sighed. Nature walks with my dad were, I was discovering, as far from real backpacking as Asgard was from Earth. I had lots to learn. And I had a sinking feeling I would learn it all the hard way.

Socks changed, we hefted our packs and marched on.

Before long, the general burning sensation in my boots resolved itself into several intense spots that sizzled with every step. Even the wet squelch of my waterlogged boots did little to cool them.

Blisters. Aw, nuts.

"Did you bring any Band-Aids?" I asked Nacho.

"Band-Aids?" he said.

Glancing down at us from the next switchback, Bridget flashed a superior smirk. I was beginning to think that was her normal expression. "Sounds like somebody forgot to read the packing list."

"Uh," I said. No point in confessing that we'd thought Oreos more important than first-aid gear.

"Or even the Ranger Handbook," said Bridget. "On page eighty-seven, it mentions that every Ranger should bring their own first-aid kit."

"Well, whoop-de-doo for page eighty-seven," muttered Nacho.

"What's that?" she said.

"Nothing," we chorused, slogging onward.

The last miles were five flavors of misery: sore, extra-sore, blistery, extra-blistery, and downright pooped. The trail kept switchbacking up, leveling off, and—just when we thought the hills were done—climbing again. My shoulders ached, my feet throbbed, and my legs were wobblier than ramen noodles.

"Stop your lollygagging!" yelled Mr. Pierce from the front of the line. "We're running out of daylight."

I groaned.

Did he *have* to pick a trail with seven miles uphill for our first hike?

Step by step, we trudged along. The scenic vistas were forgotten, the sense of adventure gone.

My world narrowed to Nacho's boots and the trail just ahead of me.

Step, by step, by step,

we climbed.

Step, by step, by step,

we sweated.

When Nacho finally stopped, I was in such a trance that I actually walked into him before I could stop. "What?" I croaked. "Are we dead yet?"

"No," he rasped in a rusty voice. "We're here."

18

Why Camping Sucks

"Thank God," I said. I staggered over to a nearby boulder and sank onto it. When I shrugged off the shoulder straps and undid my bellyband, I felt so light, I thought I'd float up like a birthday balloon.

After chugging the last of my water, I revived enough to look around. My fellow Rangers were sprawled about a cleared area among tall firs at the edge of a lake. Our campsite. A chilly breeze whipped off the water, making my sweaty shirt and damp pants legs feel extra clammy. The air smelled of pinesap and dirt and moldy leaves. The sun hung low over a distant ridge.

Most of the kids had just collapsed wherever they stopped. But when I scanned the group, I noticed Bridget and Tavia were still on their feet, already claiming their sleeping area and putting up their tent.

I nudged Nacho, pointing. "Should we be doing that?"

"Nah, they're freaks," he said. "First, let's work on coming back from the dead."

Cracking open our first packet of cookies, I passed him a fistful and began munching.

Mr. Pierce had found a seat on a fallen log and was rummaging through his pack, undoubtedly thinking deep, troopmaster-y thoughts. Xander proved he was truly Hulk Jr. by strolling around like he hadn't just spent the past four hours carrying the weight of a small blue whale on his back.

"Hey, guys," he said, greeting Nacho and me. "Want some?"

"No thanks," I said, waving an Oreo. "We've got the queen of cookies."

Nacho peered around at the other fallen hikers, then up at Xander. "How come you're still standing?"

The big guy raised a shoulder. "That hike? No big deal."

"You are insane," said Nacho, a tinge of admiration in his voice.

Xander didn't quite know what to make of that, so he nodded at us and shuffled off. Upending his water bottle, Nacho caught the last drops on his tongue.

"Where do we refill?" he asked.

Reexamining the campsite, I noticed a definite lack of spigots. "The lake, I guess?"

He grunted, reluctant to move. "Ugh. Can you bring it over here?"

Looking from him to the water, I remembered that my bottle was empty too. "I'll go," I said. "But you owe me big-time."

"Forever in your debt, sir," said Nacho in a pretty decent British accent, holding out his empty bottle.

I levered myself up onto my feet, swayed briefly, and took stock. Everything was sore, except maybe my elbows and fingertips. I grabbed his bottle and mine and began hobbling over to the lakeshore like a thousand-year-old man.

Halfway there, Frankie's voice stopped me. "Where you headed, stranger?"

I gestured with one of the bottles at the lake. "Water refill."

She shook her head.

"What?"

"Do you *want* giardia and leptospirosis?"

I shifted my weight to ease the pressure on my right foot's blisters. "Depends. Are they two new manga I haven't read yet?"

Frankie tossed a pebble at me. "No, doofus. They're infections from drinking stagnant water."

"Oh." I looked from her to the lake. "Then, where—?"

Frankie pointed across the campsite. "The stream. And use your iodine tablets." When I didn't reply right away, she said, "You did bring them?"

"Of course," I said. *Not.* Another item we'd considered nonessential.

Frankie sighed. She reached into her pack, extracted a small bottle, and shook a handful of pills onto her palm. "Here."

"Thanks." I accepted the tablets, dropping two into each water bottle and the rest into my pocket.

"Bridget was right," she said. "You didn't check the list and you haven't read the handbook."

"In my defense, joining the Rangers wasn't voluntary. It was punishment."

She smirked. "You've been a bad boy?"

I shifted weight onto my right foot to ease my left foot's blisters. "You might say that." This flirting, or whatever we were doing, was nice. It gave me a bubbly feeling in my chest, like drinking a Coke too fast. Maybe this was what Dad felt with Shasta, or Mom felt on her dates? Everyone should feel this way.

But, bubbly feeling aside, I needed to get off my feet soon or I would keel over.

"Go," said Frankie with a wave. "Bad boy or not, I'm glad you're here."

Limping off to the stream, I muttered, "Me too."

Night in the mountains zooms in faster than Superman on steroids. One minute, Nacho and I were gathering wood for the fire; the next minute, it was too dark to see.

"Where's your flashlight?" I asked, juggling my armload of branches.

"In my backpack," said Nacho. "Where's yours?"

"Same."

We stumbled through the woods, bumping into trees and tripping over logs. Over and over, Nacho and I gathered our dropped kindling.

"Are we heading the right way?" I asked.

"You know, we wouldn't have this problem at the mall," he replied.

Finally, what felt like ages later, we spotted a glow where some enterprising Rangers had lit a campfire. If they hadn't, we might have wandered all night.

Nacho and I shuffled into the campsite, scratched up and practically starving.

"Ugh, chamaco, camping is hard work," said Nacho as we dumped our branches on the woodpile. "Fetch water, gather wood, cook and clean. At a hotel, people do that stuff for you."

Besides Bridget and Tavia, only one other pair of campers had set up a tent. Mr. Pierce was cooking his dinner on a camp stove. Our troopmaster had been surprisingly quiet, for a guy who lived for ordering people about.

"What's the deal with Mr. Pierce?" I asked.

"Uh, he's a twisted monster who likes seeing kids suffer," said Nacho. "I thought you knew that."

I sank onto a tree stump. "No, I mean he's usually ordering us around. But other than telling us to collect firewood, he hasn't said boo since we got here. What's going on?"

We glanced over at his smaller campfire. Producing a flask of something, Mr. Pierce took a swig and gazed up into the trees.

"Beats me," said Nacho. "Grown-ups are a mystery. But I've got a more important question."

"What's that?"

"What's for dinner?"

A few kids had broken out their camp stoves and were already cooking over them. Others, like Frankie, Xander, and Kelvin, had rigged their pots at the edge of the main campfire. Since Mom hadn't wanted to spring for a fancy stove, we'd be campfire cookers too. I dug into my backpack.

"Let's see, how about franks and beans?" I said, hefting two cans of baked beans.

"You kidding?" said Nacho. "I'm hungry enough to eat the can."

Shuffling on our sore feet like two old men, we dug out the buns, hot dogs, pot, and plates. I had a "duh" moment when I thought we'd forgotten to bring a can opener. But then I remembered my brand-new Swiss Army knife—good ol' Mom—and used its attachment to open the cans and dump the beans into a pot.

We joined the crew around the campfire. "It's alive!" joked Kelvin as we lumbered into the circle of firelight.

"Ha, ha," said Nacho. "I don't notice you dancing the boogaloo."

Kelvin made a rueful face. "I may never walk again." He brightened. "But hey, I've got fixings for s'mores later."

"See?" Frankie said, lowering her voice. "Those matches came in handy, and Pierce didn't suspect a thing."

Sure enough, our troopmaster was reading a book by firelight, as chill as a penguin's pantry.

Following the lead of our fellow Rangers, we balanced our pot on two rocks at the edge of the fire, speared our hot dogs on shish kebab skewers, and held them over the flames. We passed a bag of tortilla chips around, and everyone took some. For a little while, the only sound was the crackle of the fire and the occasional pop of the sap as the wood burned. The smoky smell was almost comforting.

"Ah, this is the life," said Kelvin, staring into the fire.

I glanced around at the orangey light flickering off tree trunks, and up at the stars twinkling between branches. "You're not wrong."

"You're both crazy," said Nacho. "I'd give my right arm right now for my Xbox and a pizza with everything."

"Mmm, pizza," said Xander.

We gazed into the flames, watching our dinner cook. The smell of our various meals—hot dogs, chili mac, beans, and Indian food—rose through the cool night air. My belly rumbled.

"You know," said Frankie, "I feel like we earned this."

"How do you mean?" I asked.

She lifted a shoulder. "After that long drive and tough hike."

"Tough hike? Thought it was a breeze for you."

Frankie grinned. "Never let 'em see you sweat. Anyway, we earned this, sitting around the fire, enjoying nature. *This* is why me and the other girls joined."

Nacho groaned. "Spare me. As soon as my moms let me, I am so outta here. Right, Coop?"

I glanced at my friend. Strange to say, I was actually enjoying being on this campout, despite all the challenges. But I felt kind of protective of those feelings. "Yeah, sure," I said. "Outta here."

Frankie's eyes found mine. Odd, but in that moment, I felt like she understood me better than my best friend. I looked away, suddenly shy.

"I think your dogs are done," said Kelvin.

The beans were ready too. After dishing everything out, most of the next ten minutes was taken up with stuffing food into our faces. We barely spoke, other than to grunt something like "Pass the ketchup."

At long last, I burped and set my plate aside. I noticed Tavia and Bridget eating their own dinners over by their tent. "How come you're not eating with them?" I asked Frankie.

She mopped up the last of her meal with a piece of naan. "Ah, Bridget is more Tavia's friend. To be honest, she kind of gets on my nerves sometimes."

"Join the club," said Nacho, Kelvin, and me. Everyone laughed.

Bellies full, we stretched out our legs and relaxed. All except Kelvin, who squatted closer to the fire, feeding branches into it again and again. The guy sure loved his flames. Before long, he'd created a monster of a bonfire, and we all had to drag our logs farther away from its heat.

"You know, Bridget's not that bad," said Frankie.

"Really?" I said.

She held up a palm. "Sure, she can be kind of an overachieving . . ."

"Overbearing, know-it-all pain in the—?" suggested Nacho.

"But her heart's in the right place. She's had to work crazy hard to measure up to her mom's achievements. That's all."

I cocked my head. "Her mom? Are we talking about the same person? The one who made us sing 'Little Bunny Foo Foo'?"

Frankie chuckled. "Yeah, she's terminally chipper, but Mrs. Click is an astrophysicist, and when she was younger—"

"Hey, guys," Xander interrupted.

"An *astrophysicist*?" I said. "Sorry, I—"

"*Guys*," he repeated.

"What?" My answer came out kind of sharp.

He pointed. "Fire."

"Huh?" At first, it looked like he was pointing to the

campfire, and duh, of course it was a fire. But then I really focused.

As the bigger logs caught, our bonfire had morphed into a raging, out-of-control monster. Its flames licked up at the branches above us, threatening to torch the tree and engulf the camp.

But that wasn't even the worst part.

With all of his tinkering and tending and campfire feeding, Kelvin had gotten careless. One sleeve of his jacket was pure flame.

"Fire!" I cried.

19

Kelvin the Human Torch

Kelvin leaped to his feet with a brain-piercing shriek. His eyes were wider than twin storm drains and he waved his burning arm like he was trying to shake off the flames. That only made them jump higher.

"Water!" I cried. "Somebody help!"

"Grab him!" yelled Frankie.

"Somebody control that campfire," I shouted, lunging to my feet.

Freaked out of his mind, Kelvin gave another wild cry and started running around. I chased him. We must have made quite a sight, him dodging back and forth as randomly as a nectar-drunk butterfly, me trying to guess where he was headed next.

Then Kelvin tripped over a log and fell in the dirt. Dropping to my knees, I held his legs. Kelvin thumped his burning arm against the ground.

"Now what?" I asked Frankie, ducking back as his arm swung past my face.

"Roll him!" she cried.

At once I saw what she had in mind. I rolled Kelvin back and forth with the burning sleeve underneath him.

In no time at all, the fire was out.

When I glanced behind me, Nacho, Xander, and a few other campers were scooping dirt onto the fire with their dinner plates. Tavia raced over with a canvas bucket and dumped water onto the flames. The bonfire seemed to be calming down.

"Ow, ow, ow!" Sitting up, Kelvin cradled his scorched arm, coughing and hacking. Lucky thing he'd been wearing a jacket, because the sleeve was mostly gone. Patches of red, raw skin showed through the gaps in the fabric, and an acrid, foul stench, like spoiled bacon frying, burned its way into my nose.

My stomach rolled, and I thought I'd be sick right then and there. Swallowing, I sat back hard on the ground.

"Cool water, that's what he needs." I glanced up, and there stood Bridget Click, the walking Ranger encyclopedia. For the first time ever, I was glad to see her.

"The lake," I croaked, my throat as parched as Death Valley.

"Actually, the stream would be cleaner," Bridget replied.

By the time I helped Kelvin to his feet, it seemed like the entire camp had come to watch. Mr. Pierce pushed through.

"Everyone, take two steps back," he ordered. When nobody moved, he barked, "Now, dipsticks!"

That did the trick. Kids shuffled back, eyes glued to the scene.

"He'll need gauze," said José. His normally cheerful face wore a serious expression.

"Plastic wrap is better, actually," said Bridget. Man, was there anything that girl didn't know?

"Bridget, you organize that," said Mr. Pierce. "I'll help him soak that arm." Searching the Rangers' faces, he asked, "Anyone know for how long?"

"Ten minutes," said Frankie.

"Twenty," said Bridget.

The troopmaster nodded. "Twenty it is. Miss Jackson, bring that bucket and follow us. This arm's going in the stream."

Guiding Kelvin by his shoulders and talking in soothing tones, Mr. Pierce walked him through camp to the water. Tavia's flashlight lit their way.

We all stood gaping, watching them go.

"Wow," said Nacho.

"Yeah," said Xander.

I coughed, trying to purge the smoke and that awful smell of singed flesh from my mouth and nose. A hand thumped my back, and it turned out to be connected to Frankie.

"You okay?" she asked.

I nodded. "Better than Kelvin. How did you know to roll him?"

Frankie pulled a wry expression. "From the source of all knowledge. Reality TV."

That wrenched a painful chuckle from me.

"I'm gonna go see if Bridget needs any help," she said. And with another pat on my back, she was gone.

The kids who hadn't been at our fire crowded around, wanting to know how Kelvin had gone all Human Torch on us. Nacho and I filled them in as best we could.

"You play with fire, you get burned," said Xander. Probably the longest sentence I'd heard from him yet.

"Harsh, dude," said Nacho.

"No, no." Xander waved a hand to erase the words. "My dad's saying. Now I get it."

Eventually, the other campers drifted away, and it was just me, Nacho, and Xander sitting around the campfire. As carefully as possible, I tossed another log on. We stared into the flames.

"Tent time," muttered Xander at last. He rose with a grunt and lumbered off into the darkness.

"Us too," I said, turning to Nacho.

He grimaced. "Do we have to? I'm beat."

I slumped, feeling every mile we had hiked and sensing the post-accident adrenaline draining away. "Maybe not."

"Great, let's sleep under the stars."

Glancing up, I couldn't see anything twinkling between the treetops. I wondered dully where the stars had gone, but I was too tired to follow that thought. Nacho and I shuffled over to our packs, unrolled our sleeping bags, and laid them down on top of a tarp. Then we crawled inside, barely remembering to remove our boots first.

Right away, something hard dug into my shoulder blade. Rolling onto my side, I searched for a more comfortable position. Beside me, Nacho was doing the same.

"Rocks?" I asked.

"Rocks," he said.

I groaned. "Maybe next time we should set up while it's still light."

"Yeah right," he said. "*Next* time."

Closing my eyes, I let the sounds of the camp wash over me. Burning logs popped, crickets chirred, voices murmured. Someone in Xander's area snored like a lumberjack, and I heard the clatter of a camper washing dinner dishes.

"Maybe we should also have cleaned our plates before bed," I murmured.

"Next time," said Nacho.

I grunted. Neither of us spoke for a long while. Tired as I was, I felt almost too tired to sleep, if that makes any sense. Just when I thought my friend had passed out, Nacho spoke.

"Just think. If we hadn't jumped off of that Prince of Pirates ride back in May, we wouldn't even be here."

And then maybe my mom wouldn't have met Mr. Pierce and messed up my plans to reunite her with my dad. But even so, I'd probably still be clueless about the subject of my graphic novel.

I sighed my longest sigh yet. "Good night, chamaco."

It felt like I'd only been asleep for a minute when I heard plates clattering and someone making a low grunting.

"Nacho, *shhh*," I said, with eyes closed.

"Mmf?" he mumbled. Strange, but his voice seemed to be coming from a different direction from the plate sounds.

"Noisy," I said. "Go back to sleep."

"You woke *me* up," he said, sounding a little more awake.

"But—" I sat up, fumbling blearily for my flashlight. By the embers of our campfire, I could barely make out a dark shape near our packs. "Xander?"

Nacho located his flashlight and clicked it on. "Dude,

if you want more cookies—" His voice died in his throat.

Squatting there in the flashlight's glow, rummaging through Nacho's backpack, was a two-hundred-pound black bear. It huffed a couple times, annoyed by the light, and gave a low growl.

The tiny hairs stood up all over my body. My limbs felt shaky and I could barely speak.

"B-b-bear," I breathed.

20

The Bear Necessities

"Wh-wh-what do we do?" Nacho whispered.

Right about then, I wished we had put up our tent. And maybe even hung our food from a tree.

But it was too late for wishes.

The bear growled, louder this time. Its mouth opened wide, fangs glimmering in the light.

"Don't move," I whispered to my friend. "Don't make a sound."

A tent unzipped, somewhere to our right, and another flashlight beam found the creature. "Bear!" cried Nate at the top of his lungs.

"Shh!" I said.

"Holy crud!" he yelled, his voice jumping an octave.

Confused, the bear turned toward him, rising out of its squat.

Was Nate trying to get us eaten up? "Be quiet!" I whisper-shouted.

"No," said Nate. "You gotta make noise to scare 'em off." He ducked back into his tent. For a moment, I thought he was abandoning us to our fate, but then . . .

Pang! Pang! Pang!

He emerged, beating two pots together. "Stand up!" shouted Nate. "Make yourself big!"

The last thing I wanted was for that bear to notice me. But Nacho and I did as he commanded, standing and waving our arms.

"Yah! Beat it, bear!" we yelled, our voices quavering.

Baffled, the creature swung its huge head back and forth, from Nate to us. I hoped it wasn't deciding whom to eat first. Then, as our racket continued, amplified by the other campers as they joined in with the banging pots, the bear had enough.

With a high whining growl, it turned and lumbered off into the darkness. I watched it go. My knees shook like a grass shack in an earthquake, and my heartbeat thundered in my ears.

After all the ruckus, nearly everyone in the troop was awake. (All but Xander, that is, who somehow snored on.) We threw more logs on the campfire and talked over the bear incident.

"What was it after, anyway?" asked Bridget.

Fingering the shredded top of his backpack, Nacho moaned, "My Oreos!"

She shook her head. "Always put your food in bear bags and hang it high." Bridget's flashlight swung, illuminating her own food bag, which dangled from a branch.

"Just what I was about to say," said Mr. Pierce, joining us. "Rangers, if you haven't hung your food items from a tree, I suggest you do it now."

"Everything?" asked Nate.

"Every stick of gum, every bottle of cooking oil, every Hostess Ding Dong. Up. Now."

He didn't need to repeat himself. Nacho and I hustled off to stuff what was left of our food into a garbage bag. After a few tries, I managed to sling some nylon rope over a pine branch, and we hoisted our food high.

By the time we finished, we were dead on our feet. Between the aftereffects of the killer hike, the human torch, and the bear drama, I could scarcely keep my eyes open.

Collapsing onto my sleeping bag, I said, "Let's turn in."

"Uh, shouldn't we set up the tent?" asked Nacho.

I shrugged. "All our food is up a tree, and I'm beat. You want to do it? Be my guest."

"But what about rain?"

Wriggling into my sleeping bag, I said, "No worries, Bridget's weather apps said this was the driest weekend."

Deep in my sleep, I had a vivid dream that I was resting on a rock-hard bed in a giant's hotel. Restless, I climbed down to the floor and padded into the enormous bathroom to take a shower.

And when I woke up, the last part turned out to be true.

Drops pattered down onto my face and sleeping bag, plinking off our pot and dirty dishes nearby. My brain felt like sludge. All I could think was *At least the plates will get clean.*

"Nacho." I nudged him.

He grunted.

"It's raining."

Nacho cursed, rolling over. "Maybe it'll stop. It's getting lighter."

But it wasn't. In a flash, it was like someone had twisted a giant spigot and doubled the flow.

I sat up. "Dang. Stupid weather apps."

"I told you we should've set up the tent," said Nacho.

"No, actually," I said, "you—"

K-k-k-krack! Bocka-DOOM!

We flinched as a fork of lightning lit up the camp, followed almost immediately by deafening thunder. After that, it was like someone had traded a garden hose for a fire hose. Rain poured down in sheets.

"Aagh!" Nacho and I screamed, scrambling out of our drenched sleeping bags.

Through curtains of rain, I saw our fellow campers tearing about like ants from an overturned anthill. The few tents that had been set up collapsed. Everyone tried to shelter under trees or ground tarps.

In the midst of the madness, lit by yet another bolt of lightning, Mr. Pierce stood in the rain like a statue.

"Stay calm!" he shouted. "Use your tarps and ponchos to cover your gear."

"But it's *raining*!" cried Nacho.

"This?" The troopmaster chuckled. "This is barely a mist."

Then the rain redoubled again. Lightning struck a tree on the edge of our campsite, firing it up like a Roman candle. Screams filled the night. Kids abandoned their tree shelters faster than you could say *Barbecued Ranger*.

"Too much!" shouted Nacho. Finally we agreed on something. He dove for his pack, ripping open the top and pawing through it. "Where's my poncho?"

The lightning strike jolted me into action too. I searched my own pack, finding my rain gear and slipping it on. Wadding up my soggy sleeping bag and strapping it onto the pack, I then stuffed my feet into my sopping-wet boots.

"What are you doing?" asked Nacho, finding his poncho at last.

"Packing up," I said. "It's not safe."

Water coursed down Nacho's face, illuminated by the still-burning pine. "Oh, you mean because we're surrounded by trees, and lightning likes tall targets?"

"Yeah," I said. "That."

"But we're not supposed to be in the open either," he said. "What do we do, look for short trees surrounded by tall trees?"

Two seconds later, Mr. Pierce boomed, "Everyone pack up now. We're leaving."

Nobody argued. Not even Bridget Click. In a rush, everyone took down their food bags from the trees, although I considered donating ours to the bears. I shoved the dirty plates and pot into the top of my pack, while Nacho stuffed our dripping tarp into his.

"Flashlights," I said, suddenly remembering. We each dug them out.

Our campsite had turned into a mud lake. Picking

up our packs, we sloshed across to higher ground, where Rangers were beginning to gather.

For once, Mr. Pierce didn't order us to fall in or form neat lines. There was no "Straighten up, you stinky cheese biscuits!" My fellow campers stood shivering in clusters, like half-drowned rats. Nobody said much. When José took his poncho and flipped the back of it up to cover his pack, the rest of us copied his move like brain-dead lemmings.

Bridget Click and Tavia were the last to join our sorry crew, probably because they had unpacked the most. When they arrived, Mr. Pierce shone his powerful Maglite around the camp.

"Everybody accounted for?" he asked.

"All accounted for," said Nate, after taking a quick head count.

"Let's move out," said Mr. Pierce. "Try to keep up."

Without another word or a "Forward, march," our troopmaster slogged off, following the beam of his light. We swung in behind him, headed for home.

21

The Art of Retreating in the Rain

What can I say about hiking seven miles through mud and torrential rain in the dark of night? It was exactly as delightful as it sounds. My feet hurt, my shoulders hurt, and my wet clothes clung to my body like Spider-Man to a skyscraper. I was cold, tired, and in some kind of stupor.

The only good parts? It was downhill most of the way, and we were headed home.

The storm never let up. It just rained, and rained, and rained—although the lightning quickly moved away. Onward we sloshed, slipping in the mud, ever forward.

At some point, the whole thing just seemed so ridiculously awful that I had to laugh.

"Are you losing it?" came Bridget's voice from up ahead of me. "Hypothermia or something?"

"I'm cold, wet, and miserable," I said. "But only one thing keeps going through my mind."

"What's that?" she asked, glancing back at me.

"Bay-beeee *shark*, doot doot 'n' doot-doo-doo. Baby *shark*, doot doot 'n' doot-doo-doo . . ."

Before I could even complete the next line, Bridget joined in. And before the first verse was through, so did all the other Rangers—who knows, maybe even Mr. Pierce? When we finished that, we went on to "She'll Be Coming 'Round the Mountain," "Call Me Maybe" (Bridget's choice), and even "Singin' in the Rain."

At one point, someone started chanting, "Who's the best troop?" and we all yelled, "Troop Nineteen!" It was weird, but somehow sharing our wretchedness brought us closer together.

Of course, that bubbly camaraderie didn't last. By the final mile of our retreat, everyone had fallen silent again. We sloshed along, eyes on the muddy trail, all thinking the same thought: *How much farther?*

When at long last Mr. Pierce's flashlight beam reflected off an SUV, we all cheered, if not very loudly. Our troopmaster had called Mrs. Click from the trail (yay, cell coverage!) and she waited in a yellow slicker, clucking over us like a mother duck. Piling into the cars every which way, we slung our soggy gear into the trunk and dodged out of the rain. I wound up in Mr. Pierce's car. I was too tired to care.

Mr. Pierce pulled out at the head of our two-car caravan. From the back seat I could see his face, lit by the bluish glow from the dashboard lights, including the clock that said it was after midnight.

It looked tired. Defeated. Even his normally rigid posture had relaxed into a slump. If he hadn't been the source of all this misery, I might have even felt sorry for him. Things sure hadn't worked out the way he'd planned.

I knew how that felt.

*   *   *

At some point, I woke up with Tavia's head on my shoulder, drool on my chin, and a kink in my neck. My eyelids felt stuck together with molasses, and my mouth tasted like the crud off a well-used Brillo pad.

"Where are we?" I croaked.

"Almost home," said Mr. Pierce. "Wake up, guys. I need you to tell me where you live."

One by one, he dropped us off, until I was the only one left. I was so out of it, I sat there staring stupidly out the window. Our town looked like one of those postapocalyptic movies. Nobody drove the streets, and everything was lit with the sickly yellow glow of the streetlights.

At last we pulled into my driveway, and Mr. Pierce turned off the engine. As I lugged my backpack out of the trunk, I was surprised to see him join me beside the car.

"I . . . need to talk to your mother," he said.

I blinked. "Isn't it kind of late for a date?"

Was that rude? Maybe. But after all I'd been through, I seemed to have lost my filter.

"To apologize," he said.

This was a new look for our fearless leader. To use an extra-credit vocabulary word, I'd almost say he seemed *contrite*.

With a shrug, I staggered up to our front door and leaned the wet backpack against the wall. But when I tried the knob, it was locked. I felt my pockets. No key.

"Ugh," I said. Pressing the doorbell, I called out, "Mom, it's me."

A couple minutes later, the door swung open. Mom's hair was tousled. She wore an oversized crimson T-shirt with WICKED SMAHT—BOSTON on the front, and a worried expression.

"What's wrong?" she said, stepping out to touch my face. "What happened?" Then she noticed Mr. Pierce behind me and put a hand to her chest. "Rocky?"

"Mari."

"We kind of got rained out," I said.

Mom's gaze took in our muddy clothes, the puddle forming under my backpack, and our haggard expressions. "Oh. *Oh.* Stay right there, I'll get some towels."

Leaving our shoes and socks at the door, Mr. Pierce and I wrapped ourselves in floral-print beach towels and followed Mom inside.

"You're still chilled," she said, feeling my cheek. "Into the shower, now."

"But I—"

"I'll get the story from Mr. Pierce."

Shuffling into the bathroom, I shucked off my damp

clothes. I wanted nothing more than to take a hot shower and fall into bed, but their conversation promised to be an interesting one. Call me spiteful, but I wanted to hear our all-powerful troopmaster apologize. So I slipped into a cushy robe left over from our last vacation as a family and padded out into the hallway.

Their voices grew clearer as I neared the living room. When I'd gotten as close as I could without revealing myself, I plopped down on the carpet to listen with my back against the wall.

"But how?" Mom was saying. "Didn't you check the weather report?"

"Of course," said Mr. Pierce.

"And?"

The troopmaster cleared his throat. "The forecast for the nearest town said fifty percent chance of rain. I thought we'd be okay with ponchos."

"You *thought*." I knew that tone too well. Mom wasn't letting him off the hook anytime soon. "But why didn't the kids just stay in their tents?"

"Well . . ." In my mind's eye, I could picture Mr. Pierce sitting on the couch, turning his hat in his hands. When I risked a quick glimpse around the corner, I saw exactly that.

Spooky. Maybe I should get a job as a fortune-teller?

"Tell me, Rocky," said Mom. Although basically a sweet-tempered person, she knew how to draw a confession from someone. (Trust me, I've been there.)

Mr. Pierce took a deep breath. "Most of them didn't have their tents up."

"What? Why not?"

"I . . . Mari, I have to confess something."

"Okay." I could hear the sofa springs groan as my mom shifted her position. Scootching closer, I listened intently.

"I'm not an experienced camper," said Mr. Pierce.

My jaw dropped. Had this guy been lying to us the whole time? Maybe he wasn't even a Marine?

When I sneaked another peek, Mom was sitting cross-legged on the couch, facing him with her head cocked. "But your Marine Corps training?"

He avoided her eyes. "Mostly in cybersecurity."

"But your tours of duty, surely you camped out then? You said you were in the Middle East."

Pierce fiddled with his hat some more. "At Camp Leatherneck." When she gave him a blank look, he said, "On base. And even when we went out on sorties, we never camped overnight." He glanced away. "Last night, when the troop pulled into camp, I . . . didn't know what to tell them to do."

"What?" I was on my feet before I knew it and halfway into the living room.

"Cooper, this is a private conversation," said Mom.

"Not if it involves me." I faced Mr. Pierce. "You lied to us."

"No." A bit of the ex-Marine showed as his spine stiffened. "I never claimed to be an expert hiker and camper."

"Oh, so it's *our* fault?" My hands curled into fists. "Stupid us, assuming you knew what you were doing."

"Coop." Mom managed to convey both sympathy and a warning in just one word.

"No, he has a right," said Mr. Pierce. He looked me straight in the eyes. "I'm sorry, Coop."

My gut felt like a pot of boiling chili. "That's *Cooper* to you. I'm only Coop to my friends. And while we're on the subject of friends, you don't know my mom."

The troopmaster's forehead crinkled. "Excuse me?"

"You've only gone out with her once," I said, waving my hands about. "You could never know her as well as my dad. You could never replace him."

Mom's face went red, and her jaw clenched. "Not another word!"

"But, Mom—"

"Cooper Kenichi McCall, that's enough. I know you're angry, but this, this is way out of bounds."

"I—"

Her dark eyes sparked. "This conversation is not appropriate. Show some respect—for your troopmaster, and for me."

Respect? I clamped my lips together. Sure, I'd respect Mom. But no way was I calling this guy "sir" ever again. He'd have to *earn* my respect.

"The campout was my fault," said Mr. Pierce, skipping over the personal stuff. "I picked a bad campsite, and I didn't supervise the setup. I thought everyone would figure things out."

Mom beat me to the punch. "These are kids, Rocky, not battle-hardened Marines. They need guidance."

A part of me rejoiced at seeing her scold Mr. Pierce. Served him right for trying to date my mom and mess up her reunion with my dad. But on the other hand, he did look pretty bummed.

"I take full responsibility," said the troopmaster. "I should've studied up on camping and taken better care of the troop. It's just—"

"What?" asked my mom.

Mr. Pierce looked at his hands. When he spoke, it was in a much softer tone than his usual bark. "I . . . needed this. When Papadakis asked me, I was rootless, and, well . . . depressed. Work wasn't enough—and I mostly work from home, anyway. I needed to belong to a group."

"So you thought you'd experiment with us?" I said.

He spread his hands. "I know how to lead. I know how to build a team. I thought I could figure out the rest."

"That's irresponsible," said my mom.

"I know." His gaze met hers. "And I'm sorry. Sorrier than you know, Mari. It won't happen again."

"You're darn right," I said, "because I'm quitting the troop."

Mom's expression flipped from sympathetic to parental in a flash. "We'll talk about that tomorrow."

"But—" I said.

"Shower, then bed," she said. "Now."

I drew breath to argue and abruptly changed my mind. She was right. This whole mess would still be there in the morning, and just then I was bone-tired. I straightened my robe and drew myself up.

"Good night, then," I said, and went to bed.

22

The Aftermath

When I awoke, my mind was blank and my room was flooded with sunlight. I'd slept the morning away. Blinking stupidly, I looked around. The house lay as still as a schoolyard in summer. I yawned and stretched—and immediately regretted it. My shoulders were sore, my legs were sore, my feet were sore.

Oh yeah. The hike.

My first thought: No more Mr. Pierce. I smiled. In one disastrous campout, I'd gotten rid of two problems: Rangers and roadblock. After all, my parents wouldn't force me to continue with a troop led by someone who endangered kids. And then, with Mr. Pierce in the doghouse, my mom wouldn't want to date him, which meant she could reunite with my dad. (Assuming I could figure out how to make that happen.)

I should've been overjoyed. I should've been dancing on tabletops.

But instead . . .

I shuffled into the kitchen, feeling confused. Barely registering Mom's note on the fridge (*Running errands. Back soon. Love, Mom*), I poured myself some cereal and slumped at the counter to eat.

What was wrong with me?

I was exhausted. Of course, that was it.

Turning on my phone, I found a bunch of messages. The first was from Frankie:

Frankie: Parents might take me out of rangers.
Text when you get this.

I was too sleepy to respond, so I checked out the rest. The second, third, and fourth texts were from Kelvin:

Kevin: My mom is mad. Might have to leave the troop.

Kevin: Don't worry, the Dr. says my arm will be ok.

Kevin: But so cool, seeing my arm on fire!!!
🔥🔥🔥🔥🔥

I shook my head. Good old Kelvin. Still dreaming of being the Human Torch.

Bridget texted everyone to say: OUR TROOP IS IN DANGER!!! WE MUST DO SOMETHING!!!

And finally, my dad left a voicemail asking me to call him when I got up. (Why do old people leave messages instead of texting? It's a mystery.)

My brain felt packed with fuzz. How could I answer all these people when I didn't even know what I was thinking? Setting the phone aside, I focused on finishing my breakfast. Just as I slurped down the last spoonful, Nacho texted me.

Nacho: Hey, chamaco. U alive?

Me: Barely. U?

Nacho: Same. My moms r on the warpath.

Me: Um, warpath not very PC, chamaco.

Nacho: All good. We're Indian on my Mexican mom's side.

Me: K then. They making you leave troop?

Nacho: Hope so, but idk.

Me: Meet later?

> Nacho: Our usual place, 2:00?

> Me: C u then.

I was glad to have some time to myself before talking to Mom or even to Nacho. After getting dressed, I decided to cross a task off my chore list (sweeping the driveway and front walk) before Mom bugged me. It'd give me a chance to think about things.

Pushing the leaves with a broom, I mused. On the one hand, yes, I still wanted to bail on the Rangers. Mr. Pierce was mean, our first campout stank, and I still hated marching around like soldiers.

On the other hand, I actually liked some of the other Rangers, like Frankie, Kelvin, and Xander. Even Bridget had her good points. And although the blisters, exhaustion, bear visit, and torrential rain were a major bummer, one thing was for sure: That hike wasn't boring.

It actually made me feel . . . more alive.

And weirdest of all, I kind of felt sorry for Mr. Pierce. After his confession to my mom, I knew my earlier suspicions were right—he was lonely. Plus, he'd jumped into a situation without considering the consequences.

Gee, did I know anyone else who had done something like that?

But just because I felt for him, that didn't mean I wanted the guy dating my mom. Things were already complicated enough.

Gathering the fallen leaves onto a trash can lid, I dumped them into our green waste bin. Then I paused, leaning on my broom. After all that thinking, I still had no idea what to do.

Maybe I'd just see how things played out.

By Monday, matters had heated up. Several parents, including Kelvin's, were demanding that the Rangers fire Mr. Pierce. If that happened, there'd be no Wilderness Jamboree, no more forest hikes. (Also no marching and no being bossed around by an ex-Marine.)

The Rangers' district board was holding a hearing on Thursday. If they kept him on, it'd be business as usual for Troop Nineteen, but if they dumped Pierce, they'd probably pick another winner like Mr. Brozny to lead the group.

Ugh.

I've heard grown-ups say, "Better the devil you know than the devil you don't," but I still couldn't decide which outcome I wished for. Since telling Mom I wanted to quit the troop, I hadn't even mentioned it again. But when Bridget tried to organize a bunch of us to go testify for keeping Mr. Pierce, I gave her a wishy-washy answer.

This wasn't like me. Usually, I latched on to an idea and ran with it full speed ahead. But not this time. I was deadlocked. So, I decided to work on doing something I *was* clear about: getting my folks back together.

Earlier that year, Dad had given me a debit card with a little money on it, to use for school lunches, emergencies, and stuff like that. I wish I'd remembered it when I was taking my parents out to dinner. But since I'd found it again, and it still had a little money left, I decided to make a romantic gesture on Dad's part.

Pacing through the family room while Mom was in the shower, I tried to figure out what that gesture should be. What did women like? Chocolate? Nope, Mom wasn't a fan. Getting their toenails painted? I had no idea how to arrange that. Fancy underwear? *Eeeww.* Flowers? Hmm . . .

I called the flower shop.

"Hi," I told the woman who answered. "I want to send a dozen roses, please."

"To what address?" she asked.

I gave her our street address, and then she asked the question that stumped me: "What's the message?"

"Um . . ."

Chewing my lip, I thought hard. It couldn't be too mushy, or Mom wouldn't believe it. But it had to be mushy enough to soften her up. And I'd better come up with it quick, before she came out of the shower and caught me on the phone. So, no pressure.

"No message?" the flower lady asked.

"I'm thinking." Would Dad call her "babes," like he used to, or would that be too weird? Maybe use her name, or just her initial? Ugh. I was overthinking it.

"I haven't got all day, kid," said the woman.

"Okay, okay," I said, "here goes. 'Dear Mari, I miss you, and I'm sorry.'"

I sat back. Yeah, not half bad. Plus, Mom liked to hear guys say "I'm sorry." (I should know.)

"And whom shall we say it's from?" the flower lady asked.

Would Dad call himself Dad? No way. "Robert" seemed too formal, "Sugar Bear" too intimate. Maybe . . .

"Love, R," I said.

"Just the initial?" the woman asked.

"Yeah. That'll do it."

After giving her my debit card info, I hung up feeling better. At least I'd taken some action.

* * *

After Mom went to work, I spent Monday afternoon hanging out, sketching wilderness disasters and half watching a video. Just a few hours later, the roses arrived in an explosion of red, exactly as promised.

"Nice," I said. Rummaging under the kitchen sink, I located a vase, splashed some water into it, and added the flowers.

Then I set them on the little hall table where Mom couldn't miss them and went back to doodling bears in my sketch pad. But inside, I was beaming a mile wide. *This is going to be great*, I thought. *If this doesn't get them back together, nothing will.*

23

Not-So-Secret Admirer

Right on schedule, Mom arrived home a little before dinnertime. I could tell at a glance that she'd had a rough day at the hospital. Strands of dark hair had escaped her ponytail, her shoulders slumped, and that line between her eyebrows was deeper than usual.

"Oh, something came for you," I said, not looking up from my sketch pad.

"Hey!" Mom's eyes brightened when she spotted the flowers, and then she frowned. "But who . . . ?" Opening the little envelope, she pulled out the card.

I could hardly contain myself. "Who's your secret admirer?" I asked, like I didn't already know.

A slow smile spread across her face. "I didn't think he . . . it's Rocky," she said. "Your troopmaster."

"*What?*" I jumped out of my chair, then caught myself. "I mean, really? He signed his name?"

"No, but a woman knows who's sending her flowers," she said. "That's so sweet of him."

No, no, no. This wasn't working out *at all* like I'd planned. Somehow, I had to get her focused on the right guy.

I reached out. "Can I see the card?" When Mom passed it over, I said, "R? But couldn't R stand for Robert?"

Her nose wrinkled. "Your dad? Why on earth would he be sending me flowers and apologizing?"

"Maybe he feels sorry for everything that happened between you two," I said.

"Yeah?" Mom's face said she wasn't buying it.

I tapped the card. "It says he misses you. Maybe he wants to get back together."

Whatever reaction I'd been expecting, I sure didn't anticipate what Mom did next. Throwing back her head, she gave a long, loud belly laugh.

I stared. "What?"

She just kept laughing.

"What's so funny?"

Mom laid a hand on my shoulder. "Oh, honey boy," she said between chuckles. "That ship has sailed. In fact, it's so far out to sea, it's in international waters."

Baffled, I looked from the flowers to my mom. My chest tightened. "I don't get it."

"Coop, your dad and I are never getting back together."

"But—"

Mom's hand caressed my cheek. "It's okay, honey. We're both completely over it. He's got a new family now, and I'm fine with that."

"But I'm not!" burst from my throat before I could stop it. "He belongs here with us, not with that flake and her little brats."

Mom's eyes got all soft, and she pulled me into a hug. "Oh, honey boy."

"Well, it's true." At first, my body stayed stiff, my arms at my sides. My chest and belly felt carved from a block of ice. But when Mom smoothed a hand over my head, the ice melted.

I couldn't help it. I sobbed. Even though it mortified me, I couldn't seem to stop wailing like a two-year-old whose teddy bear was tossed in the dumpster.

My arms wrapped around Mom, and I buried my face in her neck.

Throughout, Mom murmured mom things like "Let it out" and "It's okay."

I tried to get ahold of myself. This was no way for an almost-teen to act.

Finally, I hiccuped a little and let her go. She stepped back. "But . . . Mom, our family is broken."

With great tenderness, my mom said, "I know it feels that way. I know it hurts. But our family has changed, that's all."

"Not in a good way," I said.

"Good or bad, who can say? But you can't fight change."

I wiped away a tear. "You can try."

Taking my hand, Mom led me to the couch and sat down with me. "I tried, believe me. But things change. Resisting that only brings more pain."

It felt like something hard inside me had broken into shards, and the edges were poking the inside of my chest. "So you give up on our family?"

She patted my hand. "Never. Dad loves you, I love you."

Staring at the carpet, I said, "It doesn't feel like he loves me. He's always working. He looks at me like I'm something to cross off his to-do list."

Mom raised my chin in her hand. "He loves you," she repeated, a determined glint coming into her gaze. "Although I may have to remind him to show it more often."

"But . . . but you were happy together, right?" I asked.

"Once." Mom sighed, looked away, and then looked back at me. "When you were little, sure."

Something about the way she said that made me think back to when they were together—really think. Now that I focused on it, mostly I remembered the tense silences, the arguments, the times Dad stormed out, saying he needed to get some fresh air. A thought struck me. Maybe our nature walks together weren't just a nice father-son excursion. Maybe they were a way for him to get out of the house, away from Mom.

Maybe my rosy memories needed a reboot.

This was a lot to process.

"But it doesn't feel like we're a whole family," I said.

She took a breath, considering. "The shape of it may have changed, but we're still a family. It looks different, that's all. Bigger."

"What do you mean?"

"Shasta and her twins are almost like family too," she said. "And they all love you. Just like me."

I thought about Mom's words. Shasta McNasty I could do without. But an image sprang to mind of the goofy little twins blowing me kisses after I read them a good-night story, and I had to admit she'd spoken some truth.

Wiping the back of my hand across my eyes, I said, "Um, I have a confession to make."

"What's that?" Mom asked.

"Mr. Pierce didn't send those flowers."

She frowned. "What do you mean?"

I looked down. "*I* sent them. For Dad. I . . . thought if you guys could remember how things used to be, that you'd . . ." My voice faded. "I dunno. Get back together?"

And now I felt like the biggest idiot in the whole universe.

Mom regarded me for a while with an expression that was hard to read. Then she leaned forward and kissed my cheek.

"What was that for?" I asked.

"For trying," she said. "That's one of the sweetest things you've ever done." Picking up the vase of flowers, she inhaled their perfume. "Plus, what mom doesn't love getting flowers from her son?"

I ducked my head. "Okay, no need to get mushy."

Mom laughed, tousling my hair. We moved on to dinner and other things. But despite the distractions, I still felt that bittersweet ache in my chest, that longing for what used to be.

And maybe I always would.

Before I knew it, Thursday had arrived. I hadn't seen my fellow Rangers (except Nacho) since our disastrous hike, but we had texted each other plenty. I still didn't know how I felt about the whole Mr. Pierce situation. Still, Frankie and Bridget had convinced me to at least attend the district board meeting.

Nacho came along for, as he put it, the "entertainment value." (Actually, I think his moms made him.)

The sun was dipping toward the horizon when we pulled into the high school parking lot up on the hillside. When the Rangers board had heard how many people planned to attend, they'd skipped their dinky meeting room, instead borrowing the school's auditorium for the occasion.

Dad was working late (of course), but Mom had driven me. Nacho and his moms arrived just ahead of us with his little sister, so we said hi and all the moms caught up with each other. As we headed down the walkway to the auditorium, Nacho and I lagging behind, some kind of flowering vine spread its scent over us in a blessing.

"So, looks like they're finally going to put us out of

our misery," said Nacho, rubbing his hands together.

"Looks like," I said.

He turned to eyeball me. "Thought you'd be happier."

I shrugged. "I don't know what I am."

Everyone from the troop had showed up with parents in tow, and we filled a good chunk of the tattered blue theater seats. On the raised stage stood a long table with five chairs behind it and one off to the side. Since the stage was so shallow, they couldn't close the curtain, which meant that some spooky-looking painted trees formed the meeting's backdrop, courtesy of the summer musical, *Into the Woods*.

Nacho snickered when he saw that. "Ooh, chamaco, I'm having flashbacks."

To one side of the stage, Mr. Papadakis stood chatting with three serious-looking men, one of whom wore a troopmaster uniform. I spotted Bridget and Mrs. Click quietly arguing in a corner, and I almost bumped into Xander because I was so distracted.

"Hey," he said.

"Hey yourself," I said. "Did you come to see Pierce get booted out?"

The big guy scratched his cheek. "Nah. It's not fair."

"Kicking him out?" I asked.

"Yeah."

Nacho smirked. "You did notice that he almost got some of us drowned or barbecued, right?"

"Yeah," said Xander.

"And that he lied about being an expert outdoorsman?" I asked.

"Uh-huh."

"And you still don't think it's fair that they want to fire him?" said Nacho.

"Nah," said Xander. "He meant well." And with that, he went and sat next to a short man and woman who looked like third graders next to their son.

"Man of few words," I said.

Nacho tilted his head. "Am I the only one who wants this menace gone from our lives?"

"Xander?"

"No, Pierce."

I glanced up as four men and one woman trooped onto the stage to take their seats. "Guess we'll find out."

Seeing the board settling in, the audience took its cue and sat down. I ended up between Nacho and Mom, in a fraying seat that sagged to the right. The group onstage looked as thrilled as if they were visiting the dentist for group surgery without novocaine. Scanning their faces, I was surprised to find one I recognized: our school's principal, Ms. Jackson.

"What's she doing up there?" said Nacho.

"Having the time of her life?" I said.

I noticed that all the board members had put one of those desktop nameplate thingies in front of them. The chubby man in the middle, whose nameplate read HORACE DOOLOLLY, CHAIRMAN, rapped his knuckles on the table. I guessed the Rangers couldn't afford a judge's gavel.

"Settle down, please," he boomed in a voice deeper than Darth Vader's. When the last audience chatter had died out, Mr. Doololly continued. "We call to order this special meeting of the Boy Rang—uh, *Rangers* board of directors, Santa Romina chapter." He nodded at the man on his left, a broad-shouldered guy called Rodney Chow.

"This meeting has been called to determine whether a troopmaster, Rockwell Pierce, should be removed for cause," said Mr. Chow in a nasal voice. "And also to decide how Troop Nineteen should be punished for misbehavior on a Rangers camping trip."

"What?" burst from my lips before I could stop it. Around me, the auditorium exploded in a buzz of chatter.

"It's not fair!"

"It wasn't our fault!"

"They can't do that to us!" Bridget's voice cut through the hubbub.

Bam-bam-bam-bam-bam! Mr. Doololly's knuckles pounded the table until he went red in the face. "Order! Be quiet now!"

I glanced around. My fellow Rangers wore a variety of expressions, from angry to hurt to embarrassed. But they finally settled down.

"This will be an orderly meeting, or I will shut it down," huffed the chairman. "Understood?" He must have judged us sufficiently chastised, because he gestured to Mr. Chow. "Continue, please."

The broad-shouldered man cleared his throat. "As I was saying. We will first hear the charges and then any public testimony before making our decision."

I wiped my palms on my jeans. Sure, we had made mistakes. But punishing us along with Mr. Pierce was totally unfair. Resentment burned in my belly like a five-alarm fish curry.

"Are we ready?" said Mr. Doololly, glancing at his fellow board members. "Then let's begin."

24

Board Stiff

"Will Rockwell Pierce please come to the stage?" said Mr. Chow.

Twisting around, I saw our troopmaster striding down the aisle from behind us. As always, his shoulders were back, his spine was straight, and he moved with a big cat's grace. Mom's eyes followed him, but she didn't speak.

In the row ahead of us, Frankie's dad turned to her mother. "Isn't that rather harsh," he said, "making the man listen to all the bad things people say about him?"

"Not if he deserves it," she said.

Frankie noticed me listening, and I raised my eyebrows as if to say, *She's got a point there.*

Face impassive, Mr. Pierce climbed the steps to the stage, sitting in a chair off to the side of the board table. His gaze swept the audience. I saw him blink when he spotted my mom, but that was it. For all the emotion he showed, he might have been waiting for the number twelve bus.

"Kayla Jackson, would you please read the charges?" asked the chairman.

Our principal frowned so deeply, her forehead creased from her eyebrows to her widow's peak. Looking like she'd rather be anywhere else, Ms. Jackson picked up a sheet of paper and read in a clipped voice, "Reckless endangerment of Rangers. Misrepresentation of work experience. Poor leadership. And"—her eyebrows rose—"being mean?"

Chairman Doololly coughed. "The, er, secretary was supposed to put that in more formal language. It should say, 'Cruelty unbecoming a troopmaster.' Please continue, Ms. Jackson."

Our principal laid down the paper. "That's all," she said dryly. "Unless you want to throw in breaking the Official Secrets Act and tap dancing on the American flag."

"He did that?" asked another board member, who hadn't been paying attention. He was pale and beaky, like an albino rat.

Ms. Jackson rolled her eyes. "No, Daryl. I was being sarcastic. This man served our country in combat."

Frowning a little with self-importance, Mr. Doololly resumed control of the meeting. "All right, then. Those are the charges against Mr. Pierce. Very serious charges indeed," he reminded Ms. Jackson. Apparently the board did not encourage sarcasm.

She inclined her head toward him, but didn't look at all sorry.

"I get the feeling she's on Pierce's side," I whispered to Nacho.

"She would be," he muttered. "She *loves* discipline." Nacho should know, as he'd experienced her discipline more than once.

The chairman turned to the beaky guy. "Mr. Withers, would you care to read the charges against the troop?"

When he squinted at his report, Mr. Withers looked even more like a rat. "Ahem. On an official Rangers hiking trip, Troop Nineteen engaged in horseplay that nearly drowned a Ranger in a stream, cheated by bringing matches, created an out-of-control bonfire that set a boy on fire, and attracted a bear through sloppy camping practices."

"That's us," Nacho murmured. "Full of Ranger spirit."

"I wonder who ratted us out," I mused. "A parent, maybe?"

Up onstage, Mr. Withers continued. "If the board chooses, the troop may be punished in a variety of ways, including being banned from competing in the Wilderness Jamboree."

A loud "Nooo!" rose from the Rangers. And what surprised me most of all? One of those voices was mine. Had I gone crazy? Judging by the look he gave me, Nacho thought so.

What was wrong with me? I'd hated the very idea of Rangers and Jamborees. But now? I was all mixed up.

Rapping his knuckles on the table, the chairman called again for quiet.

The crowd settled down.

Mr. Doololly leaned back in his chair, making his double chin bulge like a bullfrog's throat. "And now we'd like to hear from you," he told the audience. "Since the board didn't witness any of this misbehavior, it's only fair that we consider your testimony before deciding. Who would like to begin?"

For some odd reason, a vibration began low in my belly, like a hive of bees had taken up residence. Ignoring it, I watched as a forest of hands sprouted from the audience.

Nacho chuckled. "Aww, poor Mr. Pierce. He's in for it now."

First, Mr. Doololly called on Bridget's mom. Rising to her feet, she stepped out into the aisle and smoothed down her skirt. "Beulah Click, your honor."

"I'm no judge," said the chairman. "Horace or Mr. Doololly is fine."

"Thank you, Horace. Look, I hate to complain. Normally, I'm a very forgiving person. I always try to see the brighter side of things."

At this, Frankie twisted around in her seat and gave me a sarcastic look.

I returned it.

"But I cannot allow this man's behavior to stand," said Mrs. Click.

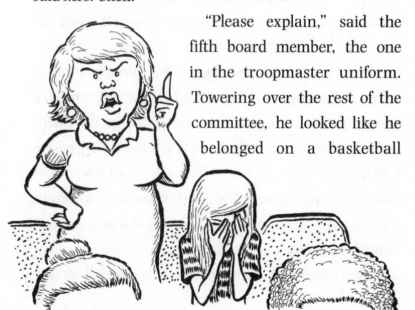

"Please explain," said the fifth board member, the one in the troopmaster uniform. Towering over the rest of the committee, he looked like he belonged on a basketball court rather than a board meeting. His uniform must have been tailor-made. His nameplate read LARRY KWANT.

Pursing her lips, Mrs. Click shot Mr. Pierce a look. "I'm sorry, but I must tell the truth."

Mr. Pierce's only response was a nod.

"This man endangered our little angels," said Bridget's mom. "It's all true. On the camping trip, he let one poor boy nearly drown in the stream. Then, at night, when he should have been watching over our children, preventing fires and bears, I heard he was drinking *alcohol*."

Someone snorted in the row behind me. "I seem to recall you like to take a few nips yourself, Beulah," Xander's dad called out.

The audience chuckled. Flushing as pink as a Power Ranger (the pink one, of course), Mrs. Click sat back down. A bunch more hands shot into the air. Next, Mr. Doololly called on a bald, sturdy man sitting beside Kelvin.

"David Chang here," said the man. "I thought joining this group would be a good influence for Kelvin. But that's not what happened. My son went on this hike and came back with second-degree burns."

A few people gasped, but I suspected most of the audience already knew the story. The board members leaned forward.

"Please explain, Mr. Chang," said Principal Jackson.

Kelvin fidgeted in his seat. "Dad, it—"

Silencing his son with a gesture, Mr. Chang continued. "The kids were cooking their meals over the campfire, *without adult supervision*." Here, he paused to glare at Mr. Pierce.

"That's because—" the troopmaster began.

"Mr. Pierce, please," said the chubby chairman. "You'll get your chance later. Let the man have his say."

When Mr. Pierce held up his palms in surrender, Kelvin's dad went on. "My son was adding kindling, and his sleeve caught on fire, seriously burning him. I call that gross negligence."

"I just call it *gross*," muttered Nacho. "Did you see that arm?" Despite myself, I let a chuckle bubble up, and Mom shot me a warning look.

"For that reason," Mr. Chang said, "I believe this man should be fired immediately. I may even sue him. He's a danger to our sons and daughters."

My heartbeat thudded in my chest. "It's not fair," I whispered to Mom. "That was totally Kelvin's fault— even he admits it."

"But Rocky's responsible for the troop's safety," she said.

Up on the stage, our troopmaster caught Mr. Doololly's eye. "Now may I defend myself?"

The round man held up a hand. "After all the testimony is complete."

Other arms shot into the air. One by one, parents complained of the harsh discipline, the unprepared kids, the rained-out hike, and the lack of family values (whatever that meant). Not one kid spoke—nobody who had actually experienced it all firsthand. A couple

of times, Bridget tried raising her arm, but her mom pushed it down.

Lava burbled in my chest. My legs twitched. And before you knew it, I had jumped to my feet.

"They don't know!" I said, cutting off a curly-haired woman who was complaining about Mr. Pierce militarizing the troop. She huffed, "Well, really!" and sat back down.

"Do you have something to say, young man?" asked Mr. Doololly. Principal Jackson shot me a stern look, but it was nothing I hadn't seen from her before.

"Yes, I do," I said. Discovering that my fists were balled up, I unclenched them with effort. "Not one of these parents were on the hike or at the meetings. They don't know what it was like. Before you pass judgment on Mr. Pierce or the troop, don't you want to hear from us Rangers? The ones who were actually there?"

The board members exchanged looks. The really tall guy, Mr. Kwant, stroked his chin. "Fair point." Turning his gaze to me, he asked, "What's your name, son?"

"Um, Coop. Cooper McCall."

"Would you like to testify?"

"*Me?*" I gulped so hard, they probably heard it onstage. "I, uh . . ."

I'd wanted someone to tell the whole truth, but I'd never intended for that someone to be me. Mom squeezed my hand. Nacho nudged me, gesturing for me to continue.

"Well . . . okay." I took a steadying breath. If they wanted truth, I'd give them truth. "When I first joined the Rangers, I hated it."

"Amen," said Nacho.

A few people actually gasped. But it was too late to turn back now.

"But over the weeks I've been with this group, I feel like . . . we've actually learned to work together, to become a team."

With a gravelly "hmph," the roly-poly chairman said, "A team that lights out-of-control fires and invites bears into camp?"

I held up a palm. "Okay, we made some mistakes—a lot of mistakes. But we learned from them and worked like a team to solve them."

Brayden shot to his feet. "Yeah! Like when I was caught in the stream, everyone formed a chain to save me."

"Or when I let my bonfire get out of control and lit myself on fire," said Kelvin, joining him. "They worked together to put out the fire—and me—and give me first aid."

I nodded. "And when some of us were careless enough to leave food out at night and the bear came, Nate knew how to drive it off."

Nate gave me a little two-finger salute.

"Lots of us made mistakes," said Bridget, rising to her feet. "Like I picked the wrong weekend for our hike. But we worked together and survived. Isn't that what Rangers do?"

Clasping his hands over his gut, Mr. Doololly leaned back in his chair. He was wavering, but he wasn't convinced yet. "That may be so. But your troopmaster was ultimately responsible for putting you Rangers in this situation. I don't know if we can allow such a man to continue leading the troop."

I raked a hand through my hair. What could I say? "Look, Mr. Brozny was a terrible troopmaster," I began. "Talk about endangering kids. But when Mr. Pierce replaced him, things were different."

"Different how?" asked Principal Jackson.

My head felt hot. I wiped my sweaty palms on my jeans. "I hated him too, but in a good way."

With a frown, the chairman said, "I'm afraid I don't understand."

I glanced down at Nacho, who was also looking bewildered. "He . . . acted mean and bossy," I said. "He made us do stuff we didn't want to, but then it turned out to be stuff that was kind of good for us."

"Can you give an example?" said Mr. Chow.

An example? "Umm . . ." I'd jumped in without thinking, same as always, and didn't know what I was going to say until I said it. How could I give him an example? But then I caught Mom's steady gaze on me, and I remembered.

"Discipline," I said.

"How do you mean that?" asked Withers the Albino Rat.

"I, uh . . ." How could I explain? Looking around at all the faces watching me, I had a swift, sudden inspiration. "Maybe I should show you. Troop . . . fall in!"

Pushing past my mom and into the aisle, I marched up to the big open space between the audience and the stage.

For a moment that felt like forever, my fellow Rangers stared at me and each other in confusion. Then, Frankie, Kelvin, and Xander made their way down their rows, into the aisle, and up to where I waited. As they fixed their spacing and stood at attention, Nate, José, Brayden, and Tavia joined them.

Soon, all the Rangers—even Nacho—were standing at attention in three orderly rows. Movement caught my eye as Bridget pushed past her mom, shushed her objections, and took her place in the third row.

All eyes in the audience were fixed on me. Swallowing past the knot in my throat, I filled my lungs, and in my best Mr. Pierce voice, barked, "Troop . . . left *face!*" The Rangers pivoted like a well-oiled machine. "Double-quick . . . *march!*"

With me beside them, the troop trotted across the front of the auditorium, up the side aisle, around, and back down the center aisle to the front. The whole time, I felt an amazing surge of power that they were following my commands—and an equal wave of nervousness that I had no idea what I was doing.

As we reached the open space again, I racked my brain for the proper command to keep us from running into the stage. "Um, troop . . . *stop!*" I squeaked.

Luckily, if a little sloppily, they stopped.

"At ease," I said. Glancing up at the board members, I noticed that Principal Jackson and Mr. Chow looked impressed, while the others still needed more convincing. But what more could I show them? Glancing around, I caught Frankie's eye.

Who's the best troop? she mouthed at me.

Of course.

"Who's the best troop?" I shouted.

"Troop Nineteen!" the Rangers cried.

"Who's the best troop?" I yelled even louder.

"TROOP NINETEEN!" they roared, grinning ear to ear.

I wouldn't swear to it, but it seemed Mr. Pierce's eyes looked a little misty, and the ghost of a smile haunted his mouth.

"Troop . . . dismissed," I said. As the rest of the Rangers returned to their seats, I faced the committee. "I didn't want to be in this group. My mom made me join the Rangers to learn some discipline."

Ms. Jackson looked like she wanted to roll her eyes. She knew a few things about me and discipline.

"I may not be perfect, but I've definitely learned some stuff," I said. "Everybody makes mistakes, even troop-masters, but we can learn, right? And that's got to count for something. Otherwise, what's this whole Rangers thing about?"

And that was it. I'd run out of steam and didn't know what else to say. "Anyway, thanks for listening," I mumbled, returning to my seat.

Mom smiled as I sat down. Nacho shook his head. "You know I've always got your back, chamaco," he whispered. "But why are you blowing our best chance to get out?"

I shrugged because I had no more words. I didn't even know why I'd done what I did.

Clearing his throat, Mr. Doololly said, "Thank you for your testimony, young man. Is there anyone else who wishes to say something?"

25

Eagle Wings

When everyone had finished, I sat still, feeling emptied out. The bees in my belly had flown away. My nerves no longer jangled. Now the board would make its decision, and matters were out of my hands.

Up onstage, Mr. Doololly slapped his palms down on the table. "Well, you've all given us plenty to think about. We thank you for your comments. Mr. Pierce, before we adjourn to make our deliberations, would you care to say anything?"

Rising smoothly to his feet, our troopmaster scanned the board members and the audience. "What can I say that hasn't already been said?" he began. "I acknowledge my mistakes, and I apologize for them. Rangers, parents, board members, I'm deeply sorry."

Mom's hand gripped mine. I didn't pull away.

Bowing his head for a moment, Pierce regarded the

audience again. "Know this: I accepted the troop-master position in order to serve. And to be honest, to meet some people, since I'm new in town. I never expected to find community like this."

His lips tightened briefly, like he was suppressing some feeling.

"Woo-hoo, Mr. Pierce!" cried a voice that sounded suspiciously like Bridget. By the time I glanced over, she was blank-faced. But Mrs. Click was giving her a stern look.

"If you allow me a second chance," said Mr. Pierce, "I will do my level best to learn from my mistakes and make this troop into something your children will be proud to be a part of. And just like that other group I belonged to, I will strive to be always faithful."

"Semper fi!" boomed a deep voice from the audience. A few people laughed in surprise. When I glanced that way, I saw troop sponsor Mr. Papadakis sitting up straight with eyes shining.

"Oh, and to answer that earlier accusation," said our troopmaster, "I keep my energy drink in a flask. That wasn't alcohol."

"Hmph!" went Mrs. Click. I could tell she hated being wrong.

Mr. Pierce took his seat with a final "Thank you."

Surveying the audience, I noticed some parents frowning and others smiling. The board members' expressions were much harder to read.

"And thank you, Mr. Pierce, for your comments," said Mr. Doololly. "We appreciate you all, ladies and gentlemen—and Rangers. This meeting is now adjourned for our deliberations." He thumped the table twice, in place of a gavel strike.

"When will we know the answer?" someone shouted.

"Soon," said Mr. Doololly.

Principal Jackson stood. "As soon as we finish discussing this. Maybe as early as tomorrow."

The chairman scowled at her. She scowled back. My guess? That was going to be *some* discussion.

Mom patted my leg. "Well," she said, "who's up for ice cream?"

"That would be me!" said Nacho.

And that was that. Meeting over. Now all we could do was wait.

But the day had another surprise in store for me. As we shuffled toward the exit, a familiar figure rose from his seat near the back.

"Dad?"

"Coop." With a hand on my arm, he drew me into his row, out of the flow of traffic.

Flashing him a quick smile, Mom told me, "Meet you outside," and walked off with Nacho's crew. Other families flowed past us.

"You, uh, saw that?" I asked, shifting my weight from foot to foot.

"I did," said my dad. "Good job."

"Really?"

His gaze held mine. "You demonstrated discipline. But more than that, you showed real compassion and fought for what you believe in. I am so proud of you."

A wave of warmth flooded me. "Oh. I, uh . . . thought maybe you didn't . . ." I couldn't complete the thought.

"I didn't care?" Dad put his hands on my shoulders and looked directly into my eyes. "Never think that. I love you, son. Maybe I don't say that enough."

A fist-sized knot in my throat kept me from replying. I just nodded.

"I know I've been wrapped up in work lately," he continued, "but things are going to change."

The word *Good* burst out of me before I could stop it.

Dad gave a wry smile. "I deserved that. Tell you what: How about we go for a nature walk this weekend, just you and me?"

Swallowing the lump in my throat, I felt my shoulders relax. "I'd like that," I said. "I'd like that a lot."

As we entered the aisle and headed for the exit, Dad said, "Hey, I hear you're going out for ice cream. Want some company?"

"I'd love some," I said. And then a thought hit me. "But I . . . think I know a couple of little girls who'd be real disappointed if you weren't there for their bedtime."

Dad's hand was warm on my shoulder. "This weekend, then."

"This weekend," I said. Dad caught me up in a quick hug and left. Watching him go, I thought, *Good thing he's leaving now. If I got any more grown-up, I'd have to shave before going out for ice cream.*

For someone who didn't want any part of the Rangers, the next day I found myself wondering often about the board's decision. I speculated while I did my chores. I pondered while Nacho and I swam in the community pool.

"Just think," he said as we were toweling off. "By this time tomorrow, we might be free at last!"

Free from the Summer of Discipline? Free to enjoy ourselves with no structure? That would be nice. That would be sweeter than s'mores cooked over a campfire.

And yet . . .

Not long after we got back to my house, Mom's cell phone chimed. Nacho and I were sitting on the couch, designing a layout for the ultimate tree fort.

"Yes," said Mom, "this is she. Uh-huh. Okay . . . I see."

Nacho's and my heads spun to watch her like

dogs hearing the sound of the treats bag opening.

"Okay," said Mom. "I understand. Well, thanks for letting us know." She hung up.

"Who was that?" I asked.

"Someone from the Rangers office." Mom set her cell phone on the side table.

"So?" said Nacho.

"What's the verdict?" I asked.

She looked from one of us to the other. "Nah."

"Nah?" I said.

"You guys don't care about the Rangers." She sat in the armchair and began leafing through a medical magazine. "It wouldn't matter to you."

Nacho and I traded a baffled look. "*Mom*, don't tease," I said. "Tell us what they said."

A smile spread over her face like warm butter on toast. "They're keeping him on as troopmaster. Rocky will be on probation, but they're letting him take the troop to the Wilderness Jamboree. No punishment for anybody."

"Yay!" I said, at the same time Nacho groaned, "Ugh!"

He turned and stared at me. "Really? 'Yay'? After all he's done to us? Chamaco, we were *this* close to freedom." Nacho held up his finger and thumb about an inch apart.

I cocked my head, thinking it over. Only a week ago,

we were dying to get out of the Rangers, but now . . .

"I think I'd like to stay in the troop," I said, much to my own surprise.

Nacho made a sound of disgust. "You're totally loco-moco. Well, not me. I'm getting out if I can." Glancing at my mom, he asked, "Can I?"

"Ask your moms," she said.

Nacho immediately dug in his pocket for his cell phone.

I flopped back against the couch, boneless. What would Rangers be like without my best friend?

"You sure about this?" I asked him.

"Sure I'm sure," said Nacho. "You?"

With all my heart, I wished I could follow Nacho. But something inside me said, "I'm sure."

I thought I detected a fleeting expression of hurt on his face, but it was gone almost before I noticed it. "Don't worry," he said. "Rangers is only three days a week. You'll still see plenty of me."

My laugh sounded a little stiff. "I never worry. You're harder to get rid of than bedbugs."

"Try cockroaches," said Nacho, and the moment passed.

The next day, Saturday, dawned clear and bright. At least, I think it did. I slept in until almost ten o'clock, so how would I know? Right after lunch, I put on my uniform, straightened my neckerchief, and headed out the door.

It felt weird to walk to the Rangers meeting by myself. I wondered what Nacho was doing. I wondered if my staying in the troop would change our friendship.

But then I shook off those thoughts. It was too nice a day to worry.

As I crossed the school parking lot, I was curious how many others had quit the troop when they learned Mr. Pierce was staying. Heading down into the lunch area, I got my answer.

Aside from Nacho, the rest of the Rangers sat around the picnic tables, laughing and chatting like nothing had changed.

Frankie gave me a high five. "There's the rock star! Coop, I still can't believe what you did at the hearing."

"What *we* did." I shook my head. "And yeah, me neither."

Kelvin clapped me on the shoulder, and Xander gave me a thumbs-up. "Dude," he said. From him, that spoke volumes.

"Hey, what happened to Nacho?" asked Tavia.

I tugged on my cap. "He, uh, he decided to quit."

"That weenie," she said. "Just when things were starting to get interesting."

I couldn't help but smile. "I'll tell him you said that."

"Do it," she said. "And let him know that if he doesn't text me later today, he's a dead man."

"Aye-aye."

I looked around. The whole group gave off this vibe like we were part of some grand experiment and they couldn't wait for it to begin. Speaking of which . . .

"Where's Pierce?" I asked Frankie.

She pointed to the school building.

Down the hall strode our troopmaster. His Mounties hat was cocked at a jaunty angle, his boots shone, and his pants crease was sharp enough to slice bagels. When he stopped in front of us, his boot heels clonked on the cement in a crisp *one-two*. "Troop . . . fall in!" barked Mr. Pierce.

We hopped off the picnic tables and hurried into formation. If our troopmaster had learned anything from his disciplinary hearing, it wasn't that kids like being made to march like soldiers. Even so, we fell in.

Mr. Pierce surveyed our ranks with his drill sergeant expression for a few heartbeats. We must have passed muster, for he nodded once, snapped, "At ease!" and we took a more relaxed position.

"First, I want you all to know how much I appreciate what you did for me at that hearing," he said. "Getting used to each other hasn't been easy. Your speaking out and demonstrating what you've learned, well . . . it meant a lot."

Frankie shot me a quick grin. Somehow, I felt taller.

"I will do my best to live up to the trust you've placed in me," Mr. Pierce continued, pacing in front of us. "And I will do my best not to call you snot jugglers or microbes."

"Or bug smugglers?" said Frankie.

"That too." Our troopmaster waited for the chuckles to die down. "Still, we've got a lot of work to do if we're going to win that Wilderness Jamboree."

Boy, did we ever. My knot tying was still pretty basic, and all the things I didn't know about camping would fill Lake Tahoe.

"Before we work on our skills today, I want you to know two things," said our troopmaster. "First, I've signed up for an online wilderness training course with Outward Bound."

Muted cheers greeted this remark. Mr. Pierce acknowledged the absurdity of it all with a tilt of his head.

"I know. Better late than never. And second, I have finally decided on our new senior squad leader."

Heads turned as we sized each other up, trying to figure out who the new leader would be. My money was on Bridget.

"After observing you all," said Mr. Pierce, "I picked the person who demonstrated the best leadership skills, someone who has the potential to go far."

Bridget's chin lifted and her chest rose. Everybody knew she would go far. Heck, she'd already memorized the Ranger Handbook.

"Not necessarily the most knowledgeable or most skilled Ranger," said our troopmaster, "but the one who showed true leadership. And for that reason, your new senior squad leader is . . . Cooper McCall!"

I gasped. My belly immediately filled with hummingbird wings. As the other kids applauded, Frankie poked me, saying, "Get up there."

Mr. Pierce beckoned, and I walked up to him on tingling legs. From a shirt pocket, he produced a small pin

with silver eagle wings, which he stuck onto my uniform pocket flap. Then he shook my hand. His warm grip was like a vise.

Xander stuck his little fingers in his mouth and whistled, something I'd always wished I could do. Everyone applauded, even Bridget—although her smile was a little lopsided.

My face as hot as a toaster oven, I waved to the troop and quickly rejoined formation.

With feet spread wide and hands behind his back, Pierce waited for us to settle down. "Don't think this is going to be easy," he said at last. "Troops from all over the country will be hungry for that prize. Are you going to let them beat you?"

"No, sir!" we shouted.

Mr. Pierce's eyes blazed. "We've got less than four weeks left to prepare. Are you going to let that stop you?"

"No way!" I said. Everyone laughed. Even our troopmaster cracked a tiny smile.

Pacing again, Mr. Pierce said, "This won't be easy. You'll have to drill and drill until you think you can't go on. You'll find strength in yourself you didn't know you had. You senseless cheesemong—er, you Rangers are really going to have to sweat. Are you with me?"

"Yes, sir!" we cried.

"I can't hear you," he teased.

"YES, SIR!"

Pierce's gray eyes sparkled. "Who's the best troop?"

"Troop Nineteen!" we roared.

"And don't you forget it."

You may be wondering if we got our act together in time for the Jamboree. (We did.) And if we managed to win it. (We didn't. However, a third-place trophy and wins for Bridget in Knots and Kelvin in Fire Safety helped take the sting out of it.)

But that's another story for another time.

That Saturday, although I was walking home by myself, I didn't feel alone. My chest was warm and fuzzy inside, and I realized my family had grown. Like Mom said, it included Shasta and the twins, as well as her, Dad, and my grandparents. But Nacho was also part of my family. And so were Frankie, Kelvin, and my fellow Rangers.

Wiping sweat from my forehead, I reflected. Sometimes a broken family can be made whole again, but in a different way. Bigger. More inclusive. What was gone could never return, and I mourned that. But its being gone cleared the way for something new.

I decided there might even be some room in my new family for Mr. Pierce. Not as my mom's boyfriend—*yuck*. At least, not yet. But time would tell.

For now, I was content. The Summer of Awesome, the Summer of Discipline, and the Summer of Getting My Folks Back Together had all fallen away.

What was left? The Summer of Something New.

And hey, at last I knew what my graphic novel was going to be about.

My summer.

ACKNOWLEDGMENTS

All works of fiction have at least some roots in the real world. This story is no exception. When I was ten-going-on-eleven, my dad started a Boy Scout troop—partly to give my friend Billy and me a way to stay connected as Billy headed off to a different middle school, and partly as a way to keep us out of trouble. Over the years, that troop grew from a ragtag band of three kids to a hundred-plus group of enthusiastic outdoorsmen. By the time I abandoned Boy Scouts for high school theater and girls, Troop 276 had developed a regional reputation as a "super troop," winning awards right and left. Before you ask, no, we did not encounter any bears. But yes, we did have a kid accidentally light himself on fire.

However, the troop is only a springboard for this story. Cooper, his friends, and his family came from my imagination, and I had plenty of help bringing them to life. First, a major mahalo to my old friend Joseph Sannazzaro, for his insights into children of divorce and how they behave. Second, huge thanks to my amiga Gaby Triana for being my beta reader and patiently pointing out all of my story's inconsistencies, as well as coming up with some fun jokes. Thanks to Steve Malk for encouraging me when I first mentioned the story idea, and to Amanda Maciel for always helping me improve my storytelling. Without the help of all these people, this book would have remained a half-baked idea. I am forever grateful.

AUTHOR BIO

Bruce Hale is the Edgar-nominated author and/or illustrator of more than fifty seriously funny books for children, including the Chet Gecko, School for S.P.I.E.S., and Class Pets series. He lives in Southern California, where he is also an occasional actor, Latin jazz musician, and award-winning storyteller. You can find him online at brucehale.com.

ALSO BY
BRUCE HALE

Who's a
good
boy?

SWITCHED
Bruce Hale

MAN'S BEST FRIEND?
MORE LIKE BOY'S WORST NIGHTMARE.

Don't miss this laugh-out-loud novel from the author of
Super Troop. When Parker the sixth-grader and
Boof the goldendoodle switch bodies, life gets *ruff*.